HOMEBOYZ

by Alan Lawrence Sitomer

Jump at the Sun

HYPERION BOOKS FOR CHILDREN

New York

Also by Alan Lawrence Sitomer

The Hoopster
The Hoopster: A Teacher's Guide
Hip-Hop High School
· *Hip-Hop Poetry and the Classics*

First Edition
10 9 8 7 6 5 4 3 2 1

Printed in the United States of America
Reinforced binding
Library of Congress Cataloging-in-Publication Data on file.

This book is set in 14-point Perpetua.
Designed by Ellice M. Lee

ISBN-13: 978-1-4231-0030-0
ISBN-10: 1-4231-0030-1

Visit www.hyperionteens.com

For the kids

1

Everybody who's anybody in the 'hood has got a street name. Some of the a.k.a.'s threaten danger, like Monster or Li'l Killa. Others are kind of playful, like Loopy or Mouse. A few make no sense at all but sound cool, like Z-Pop and Quysm. Meeksha Livingston became known as Li'l Gal Blinkie—Blink for short.

And Blink was out of control.

At the age of nine, Meeksha shouted, "Eat my ass!" to a teacher. At the age of eleven, she got busted for trying to shoplift a pair of brass knuckles at the Swap Meet. At the age of thirteen, she got caught in the act of stealing a car stereo out of a Toyota Camry. When the sixty-three-year-old woman who owned the car said, "Give it back," Blink responded, "Okay," and slammed the three-pound metal box directly into the white lady's face. The radio's jagged steel edge ripped the soft flesh from the lady's lower lip, broke three of her teeth, and caused a gush of blue-and-black blood to pour from the her gums, like a faucet turned on all the way. Despite multiple plastic surgeries, this nice old grandmother, who had only stopped in at the local Target to get some laundry detergent for her house-keeper, was permanently stuck with a smile that made her look like a demented clown.

Meeksha got away. The police description of a five-foot-four black girl with black hair and a light-colored short-sleeved T-shirt only matched about 300,000 other young women in the area.

Not only didn't Meeksha get popped by the po-po for her crime, she bragged about it. The attempted theft had been her first real mission, her first chance to prove that she was down for the 'hood. Obviously, she was.

Someone passed Meeksha a hit of weed.

"So what's it gonna be?" a raspy voice asked in a tone of approval. It was late at night on the back stoop of an abandoned house.

The question was simple. For a girl, there were two ways to join a gang. The first was to get jumped in. That meant getting into the center of a circle and fighting your way through an attack by four to six other gang members as they stomped and beat and kicked and punched until you proved your worth by proving your heart. Would you fight for your homies? Would you represent for your homies? Would you die for your homies? The circle was where you proved that you would.

But girls had another way in, too. They could be sexed in. That meant giving up a piece of lovin' to every member of the crew.

"So, like, what's it gonna be?" the voice asked again.

Meeksha looked up. "Both."

"Both?" the gang's leader said with a smile.

"You heard me," Meeksha said. "Both."

Four gangsta girls started taking off their earrings so their lobes wouldn't get torn off during the fight. Then they circled Meeksha. Six homeboyz drank forty-ouncers of malt and got ready to watch the action.

"Yo, let me tag some of that boo-tay before ya'll whoop up on her," one of the guys shouted with a smile.

"Too late," replied a hardcore chola with a nasty look in her eye. If Meeksha was gonna be sexin' her man, she wanted to make sure that it would be a one-time event, associated with a lot of pain.

An overhand left flew and the beat-down was on.

Meeksha fought like a wolf. Black and brown fists and feet flew everywhere. The 22nd Street Merks (short for Mercenaries) were a clique made up of both blacks and Hispanics. Their crew wasn't about color, it was about territory. Meeksha wanted in. Ever since the age of six, all she had ever wanted was in. The Merks were her idols, her role models, her ultimate fantasy. Tonight was the night Meeksha had dreamed about. She sucked in school. Her mother was a drug addict. She had never met her father. Causing trouble was the only thing Meeksha was any good at. Finally, it was paying off. Meeksha wasn't just getting pounded, she was getting a family. Gangsta love is what it's called.

Over the course of the next year, Meeksha got even crazier. She started sniffing glue, putting in work for her crew, and getting tatts. MERKS 4 LIFE was scripted across the top of her left breast, with the 22nd Street logo just over her heart:

Merks 4 Life
22nd Street

Smoking. Drinking. Flunking. Fighting. Dropping out. Building a rep. Running up a criminal record. In juvee hall. Out of juvee hall. Doing drugs. Selling drugs. Beefing with the 0-1-0's. Oh yeah, beefing big-time with the 0-1-0's.

The 0-1-0's were the archenemy of the 22nd Street Merks. They had taken their gang name from the middle three numbers of their neighborhood ZIP code. Nobody could count how many teenagers had died in the years that they'd been feuding, but the bitterness ran long and deep. Even if there was only one Merk and six 0-1-0's, a Merk was expected to claim their 'hood and fight—pain and death be damned. The brawling had been going on for so long that adults in the community didn't even try to interfere. Random violence had become a part of everyday life, like stop signs and supermarkets.

One Tuesday afternoon, Meeksha heard the jingly bells of an ice-cream truck pulling up to the curb by the park where she was hanging out and decided she wanted something sweet.

"Gimme a chocolate Bomb Pop."

"That'll be two dollars."

"Here." Meeksha pulled out a ten-dollar bill and slapped it on the counter.

"Sorry, I'm out of singles," the ice-cream man said. "You have nothing smaller?"

"Naw, this all I got. Hey girl, you got change fo' a ten-dolla' bill?" Meeksha asked a kid nearby.

"Maybe . . ."

As Meeksha waited to see if her ten could be

broken, a crew of gangbangers rolled up, creepin' style, in a green Ford Escort. They had caught Meeksha slippin'.

"No, it looks like I only have eight . . ."

"Oh, shit!" Meeksha screamed.

"That's right, bitch . . . O-One-O!"

Pop-pop-pop-pop-pop . . .

A semiautomatic handgun sprayed Meeksha with bullets. She tried to run, but only made it five feet before her chest was pumped with hollow points.

The ice-cream man dove to the floor of his truck. Little kids screamed and took off for the playground. The girl who had tried to make change for Meeksha's ten-dollar bill didn't even try to run. She didn't know Meeksha. All she had wanted was a Rainbow Éclair.

"That's right, bitch . . . O-One-O!"

And that's how Tina Maryssa Anderson died. With eight dollars in her wallet at the age of fourteen.

2

R P, RT. That's how Tina's death was known around the 'hood. It was nothing more than a simple RP, RT—"wrong place, wrong time."

Each member of the Anderson family took the news of Tina's murder in a different way. Mrs. Anderson was devastated. Losing her baby girl to gang violence left an empty, hollow stare in her eyes. Pops, Tina's father, was equally wounded, but concealed his suffering more than his wife could. Guilt as much as grief filled his heart. As a father, Pops viewed his role in the family to be both provider and protector. Now his baby girl was dead. He had failed.

Andre, Tina's oldest brother, known affectionately as "the Hoopster" for his skills on the local pickup basketball court, struggled with his feelings. Andre knew violence: as a teenager, he had been assaulted by racists—but he had lived, and come back even stronger in the end. Reflective by nature, Andre retreated into his thoughts, few of which found their way to his lips. His silence spoke for him.

Theresa—"Tee-Ay" as she was called by her friends—rushed back from college as soon as she heard the news. *How could something like this happen again?* was the question that rolled over and over through her mind. Her best friend had been randomly shot in a drive-by in her senior year of high school, and now bullets were flying through her life yet again. *I just don't understand,* she said to herself, like a broken stereo playing the same song over and over. *I just don't understand.*

Teddy, however, the youngest brother in the Anderson family, shared none of his parents' or siblings' emotions. At seventeen years old, he had grown to be six-foot-one, weighing 195 pounds—all of it rock-hard rippled muscle. Sadness wasn't his style. Nor were hugging, consoling, grieving, weeping, or moaning. T-Bear—that was Teddy's a.k.a. on the streets—only cared about one thing . . . revenge.

Late at night in the inner city, the streets are dangerous. Drunks beg. Drug addicts fiend. Prostitutes carry blades the way lawyers carry briefcases—simply as tools of their trade. Legal businesses operate as well. Bright lights in the windows of bail bondsmen flash like Vegas casinos to attract customers. Tattoo parlors ink up most of their clients after one a.m. Run-down liquor/convenience marts that sell overproof booze, the kinds of wine and beer hardly ever seen on the shelves of stores in the white parts of town, stay open all night. Smokes, condoms, potato chips, and a bottle of forty—it's like a kiddie meal at a fast-food restaurant, except that it's made for grown-ups and there's no fun prize at the bottom, other than the huge buzz of debauchery.

Tonight, however, Teddy cruised the streets hunting for something else: 0-1-0's. This was their territory and he knew they'd be out.

He turned right at the corner of Martin Luther King Jr. Boulevard, driving his older brother Andre's hand-me-down Honda Accord. The blue paint no longer shone, rust speckled the back bumper, and the exhaust pipe occasionally spit out a cloud of black dust. But the beat-up old car blended in perfectly with its surroundings. The digital clock on the dashboard struck midnight.

Though Teddy was alone in the car, he wasn't alone in his quest. The night air was thick with the unseen presence of the 22nd Street Merks. It wasn't a question of *if* the rival gangstas would strike to avenge Blink, their fallen homegirl, but *when*. The cops were out everywhere, trying to prevent "retaliatory action." Among gangstas there was always retaliation. It's the law of the streets: *You take out one of our homeboyz, we gotta take out one of yours.*

The local media had been obsessed with coverage of Tina's death, which only aggravated the tension in the streets.

Innocent honors student gunned down by ruthless gang members: Where does the madness stop?

If Blink had been the only one to get blasted, the entire episode in the park would have flown under the radar. Gang members killing other gang members happened all the time—it wasn't even page-eight newspaper material any longer. But gang members killing an innocent honors student in an RP, RT situation—now that made for attention-grabbing headlines. The pressure was on the police to find Tina's killer as the media screamed for justice.

Teddy turned left on Elm Avenue, cruising along with one eye peeled for cops, the other for gangstas. The 0-1-0's, as Teddy knew, would be easy to find. On a night like this they could be counted on to show their faces, throw their gang signs, and stand their ground. The law of the streets said they had to. If the 22nd Street Merks had the guts to come into enemy territory seeking payback, the 0-1-0's attitude had to be, *Bring it on!* If the 0-1-0's didn't maintain a presence on the streets and defend their territory against enemy invaders, their gang would gain a rep—and then gangstas in all the other surrounding neighborhoods would think the 0-1-0's could be punked, and so, stupid as it may have been to stay out on the streets while they were being hunted, the 0-1-0's did exactly that. They had a point to prove. It is known as *gangsta logic.*

Gangsta logic affected every aspect of life in the 'hood, and noone was immune to its reasoning. The routes kindergarten kids walked home from school were dictated by it. The times when the phone company scheduled repair visits were ruled by it. The number of people who had to sleep on the floor in their living rooms to avoid stray bullets zipping through their bedroom windows was governed by it. Gangsta logic didn't just change small behaviors, it altered the entire lifestyle of every inner-city resident.

Behind gangsta logic lay the conviction shared by most gangbangers that they had little chance of living to see the age of twenty-one. If they were gonna die young, they meant to die with their T-shirts pressed, their tattoos bold, and their guns blazing. No tears, no fears, no regrets. Any conversation among teens ensnarled in the web of *la vida loca* always came back around to the same idea: *If it's my time, it's my time, homie. Ain't nothin' I can do.* Cavemen had a longer life expectancy.

Death or jail was just part of the Game in the world of homeboyz. The Game was full of pain, but if a homeboy simply followed the three commandments of gangsterism all would be cool:

NEVER SNITCH.
ALWAYS REPRESENT FOR YOUR HOMEBOYZ.
PLAY FOR KEEPS—THERE IS NO TOMORROW.

Danger sizzled through the night air, but Teddy remained cool and calm. There was ice in his veins as he circled onto Greenhill Drive, scanning the streets for prey. Suddenly, Teddy spied what he was looking for and slowed the car.

A crew of six homeboyz were kickin' it by the side of a ghetto convenience mart whose large, faded signs in the windows advertised cheap cigarettes and cold beer. Just as dogs marked their territory with piss, graffiti clearly marked this territory as 0-1-0's.

Teddy made a slow, sly righthand turn, then circled a couple of blocks so he could approach from the other direction, on the opposite side of the street. The homies hadn't seen him. Teddy killed the lights, cut the ignition, and let his car roll softly into a parking spot diagonally across the way, with the front of his car facing the front of the ragged-looking store.

Once parked, Teddy covered the front windshield with a visor, a silver sunshade that prevented anyone's seeing into his car, then sat in the dark and waited. From outside, the car appeared to be empty. But a rectangular hole Teddy had cut in the fabric of the sunshade a few hours earlier created a small window through which he could see without anyone being able to see in. It was ideal for spying on the enemy.

And the cops. The police concerned Teddy much more than the homeboyz did. Teddy had already crafted a plan for how to deal with the 0-1-0's. But he still had to work out how to execute his scheme without getting pinched by the po-po.

Teddy reached into the glove compartment, feeling for a notepad, a pencil, and a digital watch with a timer. What he needed was to discover a pattern in the night's activity. Teddy knew if he waited patiently and observed the environment long enough, the magic answer would appear.

To some people, the world appeared as chaos, a jumble of events crashing into one another haphazardly. But to Teddy, the world had always unveiled itself in patterns. It was a gift he had. Teddy didn't know why he understood things the way he did, he didn't know why complicated chains of deductive reasoning and analysis made sense to him—they just did, the way music made sense to Mozart or paint made sense to Picasso. The challenge that lay before him now was to simply discover the patterns so he could manipulate them to his own advantage.

Teddy started to note the time on his pad of paper, but the pencil point felt dull and wrote with a thick stroke. No worries, he thought, since he had another two pencils and three pens in the glove compartment as backup. Teddy always had backup. He took the planning and working out of various scenarios very seriously. Meticulous preparation, in Teddy's opinion, was an art unto itself, and always held the key to success.

Teddy reached into his glove compartment, felt around with his fingers, and then paused. Instead of pulling out a pencil, he removed a small, travel-size bottle of vanilla-scented hand lotion. The hand cream had belonged to Tina.

Tina had a variety of tiny habits that drove Teddy crazy. One of them was her obsession with leaving small bottles of vanilla hand lotion scattered everywhere. In her backpack. By the computer. In the tool kit by the wrenches on the top shelf in the garage.

She'd even placed a small bottle of the stuff in the glove compartment of every one of her family members' cars so that no matter where she went, she'd always be sure to have some available. Teddy could have sworn that he had found this bottle two weeks ago and thrown it away, telling her, "Keep that shit outta my car, will ya?" but Tina must have somehow replaced it.

If it had been Tee-Ay's hand lotion and Teddy had snapped at her the way he had at Tina, there would have been a gigantic screaming match followed by a knock-down, drag-out fight. But Tina had always handled Teddy differently. She knew that underneath her older brother's tough-guy outer shell, Teddy's heart was as soft as warm jelly. She may have been the only one who had ever seen that. Instead of yelling, fighting, screaming, and shouting at Teddy when he got snippy with her, Tina would simply smile and say, "Okay," then find a way to sneak into his car a day or two later and replace the bottle of lotion in his glove compartment, where it would stay until he found it again. Teddy must have thrown away six bottles of lotion in the past four months, yet here was another, yet again.

Teddy gazed at the small bottle and remembered how his sister always used to apply it in the same manner. She'd unscrew the top, squeeze the goop into her left palm, draw a curved line and then a triangle of three dots to make a smiley face in the center of her hand. Then she'd rub it in. "For good luck," she'd say with a smile. Tina had a great smile, warm and always full of love.

Teddy unscrewed the top and sniffed. The sweet scent of vanilla filled his nostrils. That fragrance would always remind him of his sister. . . . His dead sister.

Teddy tossed the bottle onto the floor of the passenger seat, telling himself that he'd throw it away later. For now there were other matters to attend to, and he returned his attention to the activities across the street. Soon enough, he observed one of the patterns he was looking for.

Typically, the police would patrol an area such as this about once every hour. But on this night, because of the heightened gang activity, Teddy knew that the black-and-whites would be rolling through much more frequently. After an hour and a half of patient observation, Teddy figured out that two patrol cars were crisscrossing this part of the 'hood—one, then the other, passing by every twenty minutes. Teddy scribbled a few numbers on his pad of paper. Plenty of time, he thought.

Teddy also knew that on a regular evening the cops

would have most probably stopped and hassled the group of homeboyz, but that they wouldn't be bothering them tonight, not with so much tension in the air. They'd stay in their cars if they could. The po-po understood the Game as well as anyone. They knew the 0-1-0's had to represent for their 'hood when the 22nd Street Merks cruised into their territory.

But the 0-1-0's also knew the cops had a job to do. The homicide division would handle the murder investigation; these patrol cops were trying to keep peace on the streets. That's why on a night like this, the gang members and the police officers could pretty much be counted on to leave one another alone. The unspoken agreement between them was that the 0-1-0's wouldn't do anything loco other than smoke a little dope and drink a little beer, and the cops wouldn't hassle them for it. From a cop's perspective, the only thing worse than seeing a group of homeboyz kickin' it on the curb late at night when gang tensions were high was *not* seeing them. That's when they knew there was real trouble. Gangsta logic, it permeated the streets.

Some people were outraged that the cops didn't do more in the face of such blatant criminal behavior by the gangstas, even if it involved only minor infractions of the law. More than 700,000 teenagers in the

United States claimed to be part of a clique or crew. That was a lot of teens, a lot of street soldiers, a lot of potential for war. The cops were outmanned, and they knew it. Sometimes, like all armies, the police had to choose which battles to fight and which ones to steer clear of. So, on nights like these, they could be counted on to back off. Both the cops and the gangstas had to learn to coexist somehow. Neither side was going away. Gangs would always be part of the inner city—they had been for decades. And so would cops. It was like a game that little kids played. The cops were the good guys and the gangstas were the bad guys. Ask any little kid—you gotta have two sides to play. Except, in this game, little kids died.

While Teddy observed the street traffic, he noticed a few other details beyond the police officers' pattern of surveillance. He saw bums buy bottles of cheap wine with handfuls of change. He saw homeboyz in white T-shirts and baggy pants come and go so that the number of 0-1-0's hanging out in front of the convenience store was always in flux: sometimes it swelled to nine, other times it shrank to four. Teddy also saw the owner of the liquor mart come out a few times and try to shoo the homeboyz away.

The first time the store owner came out, Teddy thought he was a fool. A small guy like that stood a good chance of catching a major beating for lipping off the way he was. "No loitering!" he yelled, pointing to a sign above their heads. "Sign say, no loitering." He was an Asian man who spoke English in broken phrases. Asians owned a lot of the convenience marts and liquor stores in the inner city.

"Egg foo yong, mothafucka!" a beefy homeboy shouted back. The rest of his crew, stoned and buzzed, broke up laughing. None of the gangstas budged an inch.

The store owner shouted some more, then turned and went back inside, frustrated.

Twenty minutes later he came out again. "Sign say, no loitering!"

"Whatever, dude." Except for the middle finger one of them flipped at him, the rest of the homeboyz paid the store owner no mind. They drank bottles of malt liquor, shared spliffs of Jamaican sinsemilla, and smoked menthol cigarettes, whose sharp, stinging mint flavor poisoned their lungs deliciously.

"No loitering!" the store owner said again. Not a one of them listened. Again, he went back inside.

And yet again, twenty minutes later, he came back out. "No loitering!"

The second time he had reprimanded the homies, Teddy had thought the Asian guy wasn't just a fool, but a hardheaded fool. But his coming out a third time meant he'd probably come out a fourth and a fifth and a sixth time, too. Teddy began to wonder if this guy was just plain suicidal. The shop was his property, but if he pushed his luck too far, he might get seriously hurt. After all, these weren't elementary-school kids he was dealing with. These were dangerous, felonious, fully grown teens under the influence of drugs and alcohol who were probably carrying loaded weapons. Yet the guy kept coming out and yelling at them. Why?

There was only one explanation, Teddy thought: the good old-fashioned American Dream. This store owner was obviously an immigrant—either from China or Korea or the Philippines—who had come to the United States to follow his yellow brick road. Doubtless he'd taken many risks, saved his money, and worked bone-aching hours, fourteen or sixteen hours a day, seven days a week, year after year, just to get to this point in his life. And what did he have to show for it? A bunch of teenage gangstas laughing at him, making egg foo yong jokes.

As Teddy sat in his car, he began to feel admiration for this man, for standing up for himself regardless of the potential physical peril he might face.

"No loitering!" the store owner shouted again.

"What? We're just kickin' it."

"Go kick somewhere else. You scare off customers."

"Fool, we are yo' customers," one of the homeboyz said, laughing. "Now get your sweet-and-sour ass back inside before I go Bruce Lee on you." The homeboy threw a wild karate chop into the air, then relit his spliff. Two of his other homies chuckled. The store owner said something in his native language—probably a curse—and once again stormed back inside.

Teddy felt an itch to get out of his car and go deal with the situation he had come to deal with right at that very moment, but he held back. He knew that emotion was not the right thing to guide him. Emotion led to erratic behavior. Emotion led to weakness. Emotion led to failure. Logic, reason, and ice-cold, dispassionate judgment were Teddy's tools for success. Teddy took three slow, deep breaths through his nostrils and relaxed the grip on his pencil. Be patient, he thought. Then strike without mercy when the moment is right.

The right moment arrived twenty-seven minutes later.

3

A forty-three-year-old woman wearing a brown waitress uniform hastily pulled her car up in front of the convenience mart. The yellow name badge on her chest identified her as an employee of Denny's restaurant. Her name was BETTY.

Betty, it appeared, was in such a rush to get in and out of the convenience store that it wasn't until she had pulled into a parking space and turned off the engine that she noticed the homeboyz by the broken pay phone. Suddenly, Betty faced a dilemma. Should she take the risk and continue inside, or restart her car and drive down the block another mile or so until she found a safer place to buy a pack of smokes?

In this neighborhood, Betty knew, she wasn't guaranteed to find a safer place a mile or two down the road. She was just itching for a cigarette after a long shift at work. Besides, this was her neighborhood, too, and if she wanted to run into the local convenience store to grab a pack of smokes, she should be allowed to without feeling threatened. Couldn't a person simply buy a pack of cigarettes anymore without fearing assault?

Betty got out of her car and entered the mini-mart. No problem. But when she walked back to her car, she heard a raspy voice. "Yo . . . can I getta butt?"

Engaging in conversation could lead to trouble. But avoiding conversation might be taken as a sign of disrespect and also could lead to trouble. All Betty wanted to do was go home, get out of her waitress uniform, which smelled like fried eggs, and take a shower. "Look, I don't want any problems," she said.

"Why you be thinkin' I'm gonna give ya problems?" answered a short, fat gangsta. He grabbed her cigarettes. "Now I'm gonna take da' whole damn pack."

Betty froze with fear.

"Fool, give dem back to her," demanded a taller gangsta with his hair in cornrows. The taller gangsta took the pack of cigarettes from his shorter, fatter homeboy, then returned them to the waitress.

"Sorry for any inconvenience, ma'am," the taller gangsta said. "I love Denny's, especially the Grand Slam breakfast. Tips good tonight?"

Betty tried to smile but the fear broke through. "Just okay," she responded quietly.

"Just okay?" he asked with a slight tilt of his head and a look of kindness in his eyes.

"Yeah," she said, softening. "Okay, I guess."

The gangsta smiled. "Then give 'em the fuck up," he commanded.

Betty raised her head and looked up into the tall gangsta's street-hardened face. She saw no emotion, only coldness in his glare. *Do not make me ask again.*

Without a word, Betty reached into her purse and took out thirty-seven dollars, the grand total of her tips after working a seven-hour shift. She handed him the money and waited. Was there to be more than just robbery? Assault? Rape? Murder?

The tall gangsta paused, looking Betty up and down, side to side. "You can keep those," he finally said, pointing to her pack of cigarettes. A moment later the tall gangsta turned, crossed to his short, fat friend, and handed him the messy wad of cash.

"Here ya go, nigga. Now you can go buy your own smokes."

The whole crew of homeboyz burst out laughing. Betty jumped into her car and quickly drove off, seven hours of work gone in less than thirty seconds.

"Hey, maybe I should let the ho taste my"—one of the homeboyz grabbed his crotch—"Grand Slam breakfast."

"Fool, you ain't even got a Happy Meal between yo' legs."

"Your mama got a Happy Meal between her legs."

"Yo, screw that. I'm-a go to Tonee's to get me a chili-cheeseburger. Who wants one?"

Two minutes later, the crew of seven homeboyz was cut to three as four of the gangstas headed off for a late-night munchie session at Tonee's Big Burger Palace, courtesy of Betty.

Teddy looked at his digital watch and waited. Six minutes later, right on schedule, a black-and-white police cruiser slowly rolled down the street, turned right at the corner, and disappeared into the darkness. Teddy waited another few seconds to be sure the cop had vanished, then exited his car, crossed the street, and walked toward the convenience mart. It was time.

A gangsta with an evil glare stood up as soon as he saw Teddy emerge from the shadows and blocked Teddy's path to the store's entrance. "Where you claim, homeboy?" the gangsta snarled, stepping up to Teddy.

Teddy played it cool and offered respect by keeping his eyes low and issuing no sense of challenge or threat. "Naw, I don't roll nowhere," Teddy replied in a low voice.

"He said, where you claim, fool?" snapped a second gangsta, the biggest of the three homeboyz who were still left. Though the baby fat around his cheeks revealed that this boy was still a teenager, when he rose to his feet, he stood six foot three, and must have weighed 250 pounds, easy—a giant of a boy.

The challenge had been issued. If Teddy was a gangbanger, he would have to say something. But if he wasn't, if he kept his eyes low and offered the proper respect, there was a chance they'd let him roll through. A small chance, but a chance nonetheless.

"Don't claim nowhere, homes. Just new to the 'hood and lookin' for a hit of weed. Maybe ya'll can help me out?" Teddy reached into his pocket and flashed a fifty-dollar bill. The sight of the fifty caused the kids' eyes to light up. "I just want to score some smoke, ya know? Can you hook a fella' up?"

"Yeah, we'll hook you up, homie," the smallest of the three homeboyz answered, looking around to make sure the coast was clear. "Right over here," the small homeboy said, motioning toward the side alley. "Right over here, we'll hook ya' up good."

The short gangsta proceeded to lead Teddy around the corner to the side of the convenience mart where the grass was dying from neglect and patches of dirt were littered with empty beer cans and broken pieces of wood. Though there wasn't much light, Teddy spotted a used hypodermic needle. A rat scurried away when it heard them approaching.

The two other homeboyz paused, scoped the streets behind them, and then followed Teddy and the small guy around the side of the building. It was gonna be three against one—hardly fair odds.

Hardly fair for the homeboyz, that is. They had no idea who they were messing with.

4

The 0-1-0's made eye contact with one another, preparing to strike. Suddenly, Teddy reached into his other pocket.

"Yo, maybe you boyz got some use for this, too?"

Teddy pulled another fifty-dollar bill from his pocket, but this one was folded up into a small pouch. The gangstas hesitated.

Teddy slowly unfolded the cash, watching the gangstas' eyes, all riveted on its contents. "Like maybe y'all want to make a trade or somethin' somethin'?" Teddy asked. "Being new 'round here, I got a whole bunch of this, and let me tell ya, fools be makin' large dolla billz off of it where I come from."

Teddy slowly and methodically unfolded the bill, careful not to spill a grain of its contents. "It's the sweet stuff right here," Teddy added, building their excitement. A crystalline white powder appeared. Each of the gangstas stared. "Homies be chargin' three hundred a gram for this back on my block, and peeps be buyin' it all night long, seven days a week."

Teddy held the white powder in the center of the circle so each of the homeboyz could take a good look. The midsize gangsta, the one who had first stepped up to Teddy, smiled. Teddy noted that he had a broken front tooth.

"Back in my corner, fools be wipin' their ass with fifties, they got so many," Teddy added. He knew that by flashing two fifty-dollar bills he had started the gangstas' greed glands salivating. Now it was time to study their reactions carefully. By observing which of the three homeboyz took the lead, Teddy could identify the one who would be most hardcore, the one least likely to fold in the face of heat. The ones who boasted and made a big show of claiming their 'hood—they were never the shot-callers, always the followers. And followers, Teddy knew, could be cracked. The question was, who was who?

Each of the homeboyz stared at the powder as if transfixed. Teddy watched to see who made the call. The small, skinny kid seemed to be the one for whom the others waited. Teddy looked him over. The small gangsta wore three shiny earrings in his left earlobe and a small gold piercing in his nose. The nasal stud gave him a particularly menacing look.

Scanning the other two homeboyz, Teddy sensed that the gangsta with the broken tooth was neither the leader nor the follower, just a middle-type soldier. As Teddy scoped him out they made eye contact. Broken Tooth smiled, his look saying, *Damn, we just caught the sucker of the century.* Teddy smiled back, thinking, *If you only knew.*

Before acting, though, Teddy wanted to make extra sure that he knew who was who, so he added another serving of bloody bait to the water, like a shark fisherman throwing an extra bucket of chum into the ocean.

"It's yours, my gift," Teddy added tauntingly, "that is, if I'm dealin' with the real men I need to be dealin' with 'round this 'hood."

"Shee-it, this O-One-O territory, homeboy," replied the baby-faced gangsta, the kid who was the size of a small mountain.

A moment later, the oversize homeboy started throwing up gang signs, his fingers zipping and popping and flipping and dancing like a felonious pianist playing a killa concerto in the air. "Don't nobody be messin' with us niggas on deese blocks."

Teddy smiled. He had his man. And, according to his watch, he also had at least eleven minutes left before the po-po did another loop. "Check it out, homes, top-quality stuff," Teddy offered again, extending his arm forward to show their leader his dust.

The small, skinny kid stepped forward to get a closer look. Teddy knew that every gangsta thought of himself as a businessman extraordinaire. In the 'hood every homeboy has seen the movie *Scarface* about ten thousand times, and they all thought themselves kingpin smart.

Selling white powder led to drinking champagne, relaxing by the side of pools, sexin' up hot girls, owning Ferraris and dressing in silk suits—all while getting respect and juice from every angle on the street. Life would be like a music video.

Teddy knew there was virtually no limit to what a mere one-hundred dollars could do to the fantasy-driven psyche of a teenage gangbanger, and he played it for all it was worth. "Go 'head, check it, homie," Teddy said, extending his arm a bit farther. "It's the real deal."

As the small kid leaned forward, Teddy blew the dust into his eyes. It wasn't PCP—it was DHC, dihydrocapsaicin, the base ingredient in pepper spray.

"A-a-a-a-a-a-argh!" The homeboy dropped to the ground, screaming.

Before the gangsta with the broken tooth could react, Teddy went low to his stomach, then high to his neck with a chop to his windpipe. The broken-tooth gangsta crumpled to the ground, desperately gasping for air.

The beefy gangsta who had been spinning and

throwing up gang signs was stunned by the surprise attack and slow to make his first move. Teddy was quick—too quick—and in a flash, pulled a gun from his waistband behind his back and put it to the giant homeboy's head. "Don't even fucking think about it," Teddy said. The homeboy froze.

In less than two seconds, Teddy had crippled two out of three of his opponents and captured the third in a blur of speed and precision. The beefy gangsta made no move to fight. His eyes went as big and white as saucers of milk. Teddy was right. Physically, he might have been the biggest, but with a gun to his head and his homeboyz taken out, this kid was very much the one with the smallest heart. Panic filled his eyes.

"What's your name?" Teddy asked. The monster gangsta didn't respond. He just stared at the skinny kid wriggling on the ground, screaming and clutching his face. Teddy shoved the gun more aggressively against the homeboy's temple. "I said, 'What is your name?'"

"Beast."

"Not your street name. Your real name."

"Uh . . . Joseph."

"Okay, Joseph, down!" Teddy kicked out the back of Joseph's knees so that the boy instantly dropped to the pavement.

"Ouch!"

"Shut up! School's in session, Joseph. Time for a quiz."

Teddy took a step back, withdrew a small object from his pocket, and threw it hard against Joseph's chest, where it exploded. It was a balloon filled with clear liquid, which dripped down Joseph's white T-shirt and began to soak into his jeans. "Smell that, Joseph? It's kerosene."

A confused look crossed Joseph's face. A moment later Teddy pulled a steel-cased lighter from his pocket and with a click, flicked open the top. Suddenly, everything became clear to the large gangsta. His eyes got huge.

"I want a name, Joseph. Who blasted Blink the Merk?"

Joseph, filled with fear, looked over at his two homeboyz. His broken-toothed partner was still gasping for breath, and the third boy continued to scream in agony, rolling on the ground.

"Don't worry, if the paramedics give him a saline flush within the next two hours he won't lose his eyesight. But you, on the other hand . . ." Teddy clicked the lighter and an orange flame appeared. "If you don't tell me what I want to know, I'm gonna melt the black flesh off your bones. Now, the question is simple. Joseph, who was the shooter?"

"Who . . . Who the hell are you, dude?"

"One . . ."

Seized by panic, Joseph began to tremble. "I . . . I don't know nothin', man."

"Two . . ." said Teddy, not a hint of mercy in his eyes.

"I'm tellin' you, I don't know nothin'. It wasn't O-One-O."

"Two and a half . . ." Teddy said as he moved the flame closer to the corner of Joseph's wet T-shirt. "Don't lie to me, Joseph. Everyone knows it was O-One-O."

"Please!" Joseph begged. "Please! I swear to God. Don't do it! It wasn't O-One-O!"

Joseph's tough-guy mask had all but vanished, leaving in its place the soft features of an overweight teenage boy begging for his life. Many homeboyz were like that. Separate them from their crew, challenge them directly, show no fear, and you'd expose these thugs for what they really were: frightened little punks who liked to push people around. Heat, as Teddy knew, would make a fool crumble.

Teddy looked the homeboy dead in the eye. "You rob. You terrorize. You kill. Let me tell you something, Joseph," he said as he leaned in with the flame, "you chose the wrong lifestyle."

"Yo man, please! Don't—"

"And the world ain't gonna miss you. Not one bit. Peace out, homeboy."

Teddy reached for the wet corner of Joseph's T-shirt.

"Put down gun! Now!"

Teddy froze. No way that was eleven minutes, he thought. He slowly turned his head.

It was the convenience store owner—and he had a gun.

"Put down gun now. I shoot. I will shoot."

"Just chill, dude," Teddy answered in a calm, even tone. "This has nothing to do with you."

"I run respectable business. I sick you punks. I sick you punky punks. You ruin my shop."

The store owner sweated and twitched. Teddy could tell by his unsteady hand that he'd never held a gun on anyone before, much less shot a person.

"Back away! I already call cops," the store owner barked. "Back away."

Teddy stared deep into the store owner's eyes. He saw fear and uncertainty.

"Go back to your store, old man. This has nothing to do with you."

"You ruin my store. You ruin my business," he repeated. "Put down gun now."

Teddy quickly did the calculations and an easy answer appeared. A swift fireman's roll to his left into a fast crouch for cover behind the green metal garbage Dumpster, a fraction of a second to target, and three shots—two to the body, one to the head. The store owner would be dead before he even hit the ground.

True, Teddy thought, the store owner would most likely squeeze off the first shot, but he was shaking so much that even if he did fire, there was a good chance he'd miss, especially since Teddy's own speed would take the man by surprise. With no cover, his lack of confidence, and three shots returned in exchange for his one, the old man was bound to lose.

Joseph looked up. Suddenly, those egg foo yong jokes from forty minutes earlier weren't very funny.

Teddy's eyes narrowed. His gaze focused. The store owner twitched. The moment seemed frozen in time.

Teddy flipped over the metal cap of the lighter and extinguished the flame. No, Teddy thought, and set down his gun. It's not why I came. Teddy kicked his weapon toward the store owner, raised his hands, then looked at Joseph. There'll be another day, Teddy thought. Another day.

A moment later, sirens screamed in the distance. Two minutes after that, Teddy had five police officers pointing their guns at him. He was under arrest.

5

The cops assumed Teddy was just another gang-banger from the 'hood, armed and dangerous. They were right about the armed and dangerous part.

"Hands in the air!"

"Walk back three steps!"

"On your knees!"

Teddy followed each of the orders to a tee. He'd have his revenge, of that he was sure, but for now he had no option but to do exactly as the cops demanded.

A police officer patted Teddy down. Back of the neck, over the arms, around the waist, through the groin. While being frisked, the cop conked Teddy in the balls just to let him know who was in charge, then continued down his legs, first right, then left.

"Well, what have we here?" remarked the police officer. The cop tore a hidden gun from the inside of Teddy's left calf, the duct tape ripping Teddy's leg hairs straight from the skin. "I wonder what else we got?"

The cop patted Teddy down further and found a butterfly knife strapped to the outside of his left forearm, concealed under his sleeve. With a karatelike twist, spin, and flick, the officer flipped open the weapon. Point to handle, it was an eight-inch blade. "You heading to Vietnam or something, homeboy?"

Teddy didn't answer. He knew that anything he said could be used against him in a court of law.

There was a second blade, too, a four-inch, black-handled buck knife in his back pocket, and a backup balloon filled with kerosene. The grand total of Teddy's arsenal stood at two guns, a half-pint of kerosene, a buck knife, a windproof lighter, and a butterfly knife with a blade long enough to gut a deer. Not to mention the already used pouch of dihydrocapsaicin and the other kerosene balloon. Though he had never been a Boy Scout, Teddy believed in their motto: Be prepared. He certainly had been prepared for this mission. Except for the store owner, Teddy thought, as handcuffs were applied to his wrists. I should have seen that coming.

After Teddy had sat for twenty minutes cuffed on the curb, another cop approached him wearing white rubber gloves, the kind that cops use to protect themselves from germs when handling people with open wounds.

"Where do we stand?" asked the officer who was arresting Teddy.

"The two kids went to County Hospital. First one's windpipe might be cracked, the other is suffering from some sort of chemical burn, highly toxic. You check this homie for any more of that stuff?"

Teddy's pockets looked like rabbit ears.

"Yeah, nothing."

"Third kid's not hurt, just shit his pants."

"No doubt. Being soaked in lantern fuel and almost set on fire has gotta be scary."

"No, Sarge, he literally took a shit in his pants," the officer wearing the gloves replied. "Do I gotta put him in my car? He stinks. It's all smushed up against his leg and everything."

"Find anything on him?"

"Small sack of weed and a pair of brass knuckles."

"He goes down."

"But why my car? Why can't Eldridge—"

"He goes down, Officer Rivers." There would be no more conversation on this topic.

Officer Rivers shot Teddy an angry glare. "You gangstas are something else," the cop said with a shake of his head. "Bunch of freakin' animals, that's what you are. Should put you in a cage and let you kill each other." He stalked off.

A few minutes later, Teddy found himself in the back of the squad car off to HJH, Hausner Juvenile

Hall, the most notorious youth correctional facility in the state of California.

A pair of officers carrying shotguns stormed out of HJH to respond to a call just as Teddy arrived at the gated entrance. A steel door clanked open. Teddy was led through one, two, then three empty, white rooms. Minutes later he was fingerprinted, photographed, and made to bend over and spread the cheeks of his ass to ensure he wasn't smuggling drugs or weapons into the facility.

Satisfied he was clean, a prison guard tossed Teddy an orange jumpsuit and a pair of laceless canvas shoes. Juvenile offenders were never given shoes with laces—it helped cut down on the suicide rate.

Every piece of clothing had HJH stamped on it in bold. The shirts said HJH. The pants said HJH. Even the shoes said HJH. The message was unmistakable: the government now owned Teddy's ass.

Teddy stared at the underwear he'd been thrown. Once upon a time they had been tighty whities, but the white had long since been replaced by a pumpkin-colored tint. Obviously, Hausner Juvenile Hall wasn't separating darks and lights when washing the inmates' clothing.

The scent of bleach rose up into the air, singeing

Teddy's nostrils. He looked down to inspect the undies he had been given more closely. Teddy spied multiple stains in the crotch area and paused. There was something entirely creepy about wearing another boy's underwear. *Piss, shit—what haven't these underwear seen?* I hope, Teddy thought as he put on the orange jumpsuit, that government bleach kills germs.

Once he had dressed, an officer handed Teddy a pillow and a blanket and marched him into the KL unit. The KL unit, nicknamed "Killer's Lane" by the inmates, housed the city's most violent juvenile offenders, those accused of murder, armed robbery, rape, and assault with intent to kill. Every sort of anti-social, delinquent menace that existed in the juvenile justice system resided in the KL unit.

Teddy knew, as he walked into his new living quarters, that from this point on only one thing was certain. There would be a fight. Fighting was a way of life in HJH. A new inmate either stood up for himself or he would be punked for his entire stay.

It was bad news for the kid who tested Teddy first. Teddy struck quickly and ferociously and ended the fight in moments.

"All right, up against the wall!" a guard snapped. "Aw, Jesus, Mary, and Joseph!"

HJH guards were used to breaking up fights—

they did it all the time—but wiping up blood and broken teeth was a pain in their rear ends, so the guard wrote Teddy up on a D-112, classifying him as a troublemaker, and marched him away to the isolation unit.

"Let's go, princess," the guard said. "It's off to SHU."

"Don't I get a lawyer?" Teddy protested.

The guard scoffed. "You watch too many movies, princess. Go. Now!"

The SHU—the Special Handling Unit—was a tough place to do time even for hardened delinquents. Concrete walls. Seatless toilets. Stifling air. Wretched smells. Even the priests avoided visiting this area of the juvenile jails if they could.

Handcuffed and made to walk along a faded blue line down the center of a pathway, Teddy caught small glimpses of other SHU inmates through the rusted bars. One boy, who looked to be about fourteen, lay bound in leather restraints on a steel bed. Another slightly older-looking boy lay dazed on the floor of his cell, white foam forming at the corners of his mouth—a common side effect, Teddy knew, of the powerful drugs administered by the prison staff to kids with mental disorders. Another boy was masturbating. Though the guard and Teddy clearly saw the boy—and the boy clearly saw that they were watching him—he continued to stroke, smile, and moan.

"Hold it, princess. This is you."

Slam! The iron bars locked.

An hour later a child screamed. Teddy couldn't see what had happened and never found out why.

"I'm here to inform you that you've been charged with the following crimes . . .

"Attempted murder
Assault
Assault with a deadly weapon
Assault and battery
Carrying a concealed weapon (two counts)
Illegal possession of a firearm (two counts)
Enhancement—186.22

"Each is self-explanatory except for California penal code 186.22, which signifies that all charges have been enhanced to Gang Related. That means, if you're found guilty, there will be stiffer penalties and an automatic felony strike on your record. Care to say anything on your own behalf?"

After a few hours alone in his cell, Teddy had been summoned to visit a man wearing a short-sleeved shirt with a striped blue tie and no jacket. Teddy remained silent.

"Just like I thought. Guard!" the man called out. "We're through. Next."

Including the walk to and from his official juvenile intake assessment, Teddy had spent a total of fourteen minutes out of SHU. The man who had interviewed him never even told Teddy his name.

The iron bars were locked again until 5:45 a.m. the next day, when Teddy was roused from his bed. "Room service. Fifteen minutes, then we're moving," the guard snapped as he dropped down a tray of food. "Enjoy your breakfast and thank you for staying with us at Hausner Juvenile Hall." The guard walked away.

Teddy looked at the morning meal, the first food he had been served since he had been arrested. On the tray lay a dehydrated powdered egg sitting in a puddle of warm water with a patty of sausage that looked like cat food. There was toast—two slices—but it was barely toasted and as thin as notebook paper. State budgets didn't allow much in the way of extravagant culinary experiences for kids behind bars, but this meal, Teddy thought, made hospital breakfasts look like five-star dining.

Precisely fifteen minutes later, just as the guard had said, Teddy was recuffed and made to walk across the connecting path from Hausner Juvenile Hall to Hausner Juvenile Court. Upon his arrival at the courthouse, Teddy was placed in the Hausner Juvenile Justice Waiting Center, better known as "the Cage."

The Cage was where all juveniles who would be facing the judge that day were made to wait until it was their turn for a hearing. There were no guards in the Cage—there was no need. Each kid was led inside like a chained beast, and handcuffed, wrists and ankles, to a bench. No punching, kicking, biting, or other forms of assault could take place in the Cage. Actually, juveniles could spit on one another; and they did. But that was about the worst they could do.

The Cage was not only a place that made a boy feel like an animal, it was also a place that made a wimp feel like a thug. Since there was no way to get into a fight—and thus get your butt beat—scrawny punks would mad dogg guys twice their size and run their mouths without fear. And without any guards around, the trash-talking and mad dogging were out of control.

"Eat me, fool!"

"Suck me, fool!"

"Up yours, fool!"

The bailiff chained Teddy to an open spot between a black kid and a Hispanic kid. When the guard exited, everyone glared at Teddy with hate in their eyes. This was how all new fish were welcomed to the Cage. Teddy scoped out the situation.

"What you starin' at, bitch?"

Teddy didn't bother to answer.

"Yeah, dat's right, fool."

Teddy reflected on what he saw. While he was sure that the Cage had hosted a multicultural array of guests at one time or another—black, brown, white, Asian, Native American, Pacific Islander, and whatever other classification of race could be thought up—on this day there were only blacks and Latinos chained to the bench. And most days at HJH were probably like that, he assumed.

Teddy tested the chains that kept him bound. All kids tested their chains after the bailiff left. When locked in cuffs, a person just has to know if they really are locked. Yes, they were bolted. Yes, he was caged. Yes, all Teddy could do was wait with the rest of the incarcerated juvenile boys until it was his turn to be escorted into a United States court of law.

"Who wants to mess wit' me? Who wants to mess wit' me? I'll rip off your nose and make you smell your own pain."

A black kid missing a patch of hair, from either a fight or a birth defect, felt the need to be particularly loud and abrasive. His neck was as thick as a telephone pole, and he had fleshy scars on two of his knuckles. Hate and evil filled his eyes. He challenged every person locked in the waiting cell to a death match, and judging from the size of his muscles and the bitterness in his voice, he had it in him to follow through on every threat he made. "All ya'll are punks. Hear me? All ya'll. I'd like to murder every one of you and chew on your stomach lining."

Teddy looked away. This kid was obviously sick in the head.

A few minutes later two other boys started a different conversation. "Yo, is Lynch on the bench?"

"*Claro que sí.*"

"Shit!" replied the kid in a tone that let everyone know he was in for some real trouble.

"Who's Lynch?" asked a younger kid overhearing their conversation.

"The nastiest bastard in the state. We're all screwed today, homes."

"Don't call me 'homes,' ya punk. I'll rip off your ears and make you eat 'em on a pizza."

"Bite me, bitch!"

The black kid with the missing patch of hair lunged at the boys who were arguing. The entire bench surged. He looked like King Kong trying to break out of his chains. Every muscle in his body flexed, but luckily for the other kids, the chains remained locked.

"Callahan!" shouted the bailiff a moment later. "It's showtime." A different guard entered the waiting cell and escorted the murderous-looking boy with the missing hair into court. Callahan swaggered his way through the Cage fearlessly, cursing at everyone on his way out.

"Punk . . . asshole . . . dick . . . moron . . ."

"Shut up, Callahan," said the bailiff as he relocked the cell door behind him. For the next twenty minutes, it was quiet in the Cage, almost boring.

Then Callahan returned. Gone was the swagger. Gone was the trash talk. Whatever had happened in court had brought Callahan to tears. Everyone could see he'd been weeping. That's what it was like for a boy to learn he had just lost his freedom for sixty-two years. Even the toughest homeboyz cried.

Teddy waited. His turn didn't come for another five and a half hours. Once during his wait, Teddy was allowed to pee, but it was in a bathroom with no doors, and his hands remained cuffed. He was served lunch, too—tuna that looked like gerbil meat.

Kid after kid after kid was brought into the Cage, taken out of the Cage, then returned to the Cage—all with looks of terrible sadness after having faced Judge

Lynch. The only homeboy who didn't appear to be upset was a fellow named Gomez, a teenager with navy-blue ink tattoos running up his neck and around his skull, his bald head looking like some sort of bowling ball that had been painted with gang graffiti.

"Yo, homes, what'd the judge say?" asked a Latino sitting across from him.

"Tried as an adult. Got fifty-four years. Twice. No parole."

"Twice? Ya mean fifty-four, then another fifty-four, all back-to-back and shit?"

"Yep . . . back-to-back."

There was a pause.

"Damn, homes, whatcha' gonna do?"

Gomez answered without a trace of feeling. "Gonna do one day, then I'm gonna do another, then another, for fifty-four years," he said. Then Gomez stopped, the weight of his words suddenly seeming to register. "And then I'm gonna do it again. For another fifty-four years."

"Anderson!" shouted the bailiff, startling Teddy. "It's showtime."

Teddy was escorted from the Cage and down a hall toward the courtroom. In his heart he knew that if hell had a doorstep, this was it.

He entered the court. The bailiff seated Teddy at a

wooden table but didn't take off his handcuffs. Not with a D-112 and time in SHU on his record.

Teddy turned to his right. Next to him sat a thin man with blond hair and blue eyes, wearing two-tone shoes. He was hastily reading some papers. Teddy assumed this was his court-appointed lawyer. He turned to his left. A man in a more classic suit with a conservatively dressed woman standing next to him were looking through some files. Teddy assumed this was the district attorney and some assistant D.A., the people who would try to prosecute him. Teddy looked in front of him. The man from the day before, with a different short-sleeved shirt but the same blue-striped tie, sat at a desk off to the left. Teddy looked straight ahead. A large black man wearing a large black robe scribbled notes on a yellow legal pad. He looked like a bear. A bear who could growl.

Lynch, Teddy thought. Then he looked over his shoulder.

Juvenile court proceedings, unlike adult criminal courts, were not open to the public, which meant that, without the judge's permission, no one was allowed in the courtroom. As a result, the gallery behind Teddy was empty. There was not a soul behind him.

Teddy turned around to face forward and thought

about his sister. Tina had always said she wanted to be a lawyer, the kind who stood up for justice and the little guy. This might be the kind of place where she would have spent many days in her career. But it was a career she would never have.

Teddy straightened his spine and prepared to face the judge like a man. Suddenly he heard a squeak came from the back of the room as a door opened. Teddy turned. It was Pops, Teddy's father.

Though thirty feet separated them, their eye contact burned. After taking a moment to scan the room, Teddy's father softly took a seat in the visitors' gallery. The firmness in Teddy's spine vanished.

"Hi, I'm Bill Chance, your attorney," said the man with the two-tone shoes. Then he turned to the judge. "Your Honor, may I confer with my client?"

Judge Lynch waved his hand without looking up. "Hurry, counselor, we're pressed for time."

Bill led Teddy out of the back of the courtroom, through the same doorway where his father had just entered, so they could be alone to talk in the hall. The courts were always pressed for time.

"Okay, let me explain how this is going to go," Bill said. "We're simply here for an arraignment right now. Today is not the day to decide whether you are guilty or not, that's for another time. Today I will do two things. The first is enter a denial of all charges. Despite what you may see on TV, there is no such thing as pleading innocent. You have been charged with a series of crimes, and what we are going to say to the district attorney is 'Prove it.'"

Bill spoke patiently. His manner surprised Teddy, who had expected the courts to appoint him a complete idiot, an insensitive, moronic lawyer who couldn't give a damn one way or the other about Teddy's trial or his future. In the first thirty seconds, however, Teddy could tell that Bill was not at all like this.

"The second thing I am going to do—"

The door swung open. Out came Pops. "Hello, I'm Teddy's father. We've not yet—"

"Sir, I don't mean to be rude," Bill interrupted, "but we're short on time, so you're going to have to return to the courtroom. For reasons of confidentiality, you're not permitted to be here."

A look of shock crossed Pops's face. "Excuse me? I don't think you understand. This is my son."

"Oh, I understand," Bill continued, "but if you're present during this conversation, it's no longer confidential, and you might end up being called as a witness to testify against your own child." Pops was about to reply, but remained silent. "And none of us wants that, I'm sure," Bill added. Pops didn't budge. "Sir, please, we're beginning at any moment and I have matters to discuss with my client." *My client*. The words hung in the air. "But I promise, I'll try to find a moment to speak with you," Bill added gently.

Pops, though he wanted to argue the matter further, wanted even more to do what was in his son's best interest. Reluctantly, he turned and reentered the courtroom, a look of humiliation on his face.

"As I was saying," Bill continued, turning back to Teddy, "the first thing I am going to do is enter a denial of charges. The second thing I am going to do is request that the judge let you go home with your parents until our next court date. You do think your parents will accept you at home again, don't you?"

"Accept me at home?" Teddy replied.

"Some parents don't want their kids back," Bill answered. "They'd rather let them rot in jail for what they've done, and I'd hate to have that come out in open court."

Teddy paused. "Yeah, they'll take me," he said.

"Counselor, the judge is ready to start," said the bailiff, popping his head outside the door.

"Coming, officer," Bill replied. "All right, let's go."

"That's it?" Teddy asked. "That's all the time we get?"

"We'll chat more before the next hearing. Come on, we don't want to keep the judge waiting."

"Hold on," Teddy said, not moving. "Do you even understand my case? I mean, did you even read my file?"

Bill paused. "Not the whole thing, no," he said matter-of-factly. "Plus, I have yet to see a police report. Truth is, I had maybe five minutes to glance it over just before you walked in."

"Five minutes? Then how the hell are you going to represent me?"

Bill paused. "As best I can," he answered.

Teddy shook his head. *This was justice?*

"The sad truth is, this is pretty much how it always is. It's an ugly system, filled with sinkholes, quicksand, and booby traps, but I learned long ago to try to do the best I could. By the way, you should know something else. If convicted, you'll most likely be maxed out."

"Maxed out?" Teddy asked.

"It means you'll spend every day of your life—no holidays, no birthdays, no Christmases—from the time of your sentencing until the day you turn twenty-five years old, behind bars," Bill informed him. "I don't say this to scare you, I just feel it's important for my clients to know what they're up against when they are involved in gang activities."

"I wasn't involved in gang activities."

"Well, that's what the charges say. Anyway, we'll talk about it more before the next hearing. Now, come on." Bill held open the door. "We most definitely don't want to keep the judge waiting. Not this judge, we don't."

They entered the court, and while the bailiff secured Teddy in his seat, Bill stopped by Pops's chair and had a quick, whispered conversation. A moment later, when the judge cleared his throat to signal that he was ready to begin, Bill returned to his chair.

Everyone sat silent. Apparently, Judge Lynch always spoke first. Teddy looked quietly at the man who would decide his fate. In juvenile courts, there was no option of being tried by a jury of your peers. The judge on the bench was all powerful, and what he said would go.

Judge Lynch scanned Teddy's file a final time. Teddy thought about his father in the back of the courtroom, but didn't turn to look at him. In the brief instant that he had seen his dad, he easily detected his deep hurt. But why is he alone? Teddy wondered.

Then he looked down at his clothes. HJH was written everywhere on him: his shirt, his pants, his shoes. Teddy looked exactly like the scumbags people see on the local news. That had to be the reason why

Pops had shown up alone in court. His mother would never have been able to handle it.

Judge Lynch motioned to Bill. It was time to begin.

Everyone treated the start of the trial like it was nothing more than a well-rehearsed routine. Bill spoke legal phrases. The DA spoke legal phrases. The judge spoke legal phrases. Then Bill spoke some more legal phrases, the next round of each ending with, "We enter a denial of the charges." Bill said this six times. Officially, stage one of the trial appeared to be finished.

"As to the matter—" Bill continued, but suddenly Judge Lynch cut him off.

"Remanded to Juvenile Hall, trial to be heard in fourteen days. Next case."

Judge Lynch put the manila folder into a pile on his left, and without even looking at Teddy, motioned for the bailiff to take him away.

"But, Your Honor, there's—"

"No," Lynch replied. "Let's get the next case in here. I still have a very busy day."

"Your Honor, if you please—"

Judge Lynch raised his eyes, stopped everything, then glared at Bill over the rims of his glasses. "Counselor, in this courtroom, I am . . ." He waited for Teddy's lawyer to finish the sentence.

"Like God," Bill said softly, as if he had heard the phrase many times before.

"I didn't hear you, counselor. In this courtroom, I am . . ." boomed the judge.

"Like God," Bill said with more volume, a tinge of humiliation in his voice.

"Not *like* God, counselor. I *am* God. What I say goes, and what I see here is a young black man with a loaded gun threatening the life of another young black man in retaliation for the drive-by shooting of two young black girls. It's sickening! The weapon he was carrying was loaded, the damage he did to two of his 'enemies' is some of the most hateful stuff I have ever read about, and he has been cited with a D-112 by the detention staff for fighting while in custody. Everything we are talking about reeks of gang activity, and you know how I feel about gangs, don't you, Counselor Chance?"

"Yes, Your Honor, but—"

"Gangs are the scourge of this city. I saw twenty-six gang-related cases last week, and four more before your client walked in this morning. Murder. Drugs. Rape. Robbery. What don't they do? I don't care if that man over there, who I assume to be his father, is the Pope, I am not turning him over to the custody of his parents until the time of his trial, because I think this boy is a danger right now. He's a danger to you. He's a danger to me. And he's a danger to society."

Judge Lynch turned for the first time to Teddy. "What, you want revenge, son? You gonna shoot somebody?"

Teddy stared back, but wisely, did not answer.

"Jesus, this is madness! As an African American father myself, with kids of my own who I don't wish to see filled with bullets just because they happen to walk home from school on the wrong sidewalk, I cannot say I find one hint of a reason why this boy should not be held in custody until the date of his trial. I'll see him again in two weeks. Until then, it's . . ." The judge leaned forward in his chair and scowled at Teddy. "Do you know what I am now, son?" Teddy didn't respond. "I said," barked Judge Lynch, "do you know what I am now, son?"

"No," Teddy replied.

"I am *in loco parentis.* That's Latin for 'in place of a parent.' It means *I'm your momma now!* And you're gonna spend a few more evenings at my house! Bring in the next case!" The judge slammed Teddy's file down on his desk.

Bill hesitated. Judge Lynch addressed Teddy's lawyer firmly. "If there is another item you wish to add, Counselor Chance, it had better pertain to an issue other than giving this boy back to his daddy."

The judge looked to the back of the courtroom and snapped at Pops. "Look at the mess this child is in. I mean, what kind of father are you? A lack of responsible fathers is ninety-five percent of the problem in this crazy city."

The words stung. But Pops knew better than to respond and provoke the anger of Judge Lynch any further.

"As I said, this is just madness," the judge said. "Bring in the next case!"

The bailiff grabbed Teddy and escorted him back to the Cage. A few hours later, he was returned to HJH.

6

Teddy arrived back at Hausner Juvenile Hall just in time for dinner. He was served a tray of green meat loaf, yellow mashed potatoes with lumps of batter where the instant powder hadn't dissolved, and string beans. For dessert, the state served a plastic cup of applesauce.

Of all the items on the plate, the dessert looked especially disgusting, as if rotten apples gnawed by worms had been smashed into puddles of brown water, then drained into a dirty cup. There was no way Teddy was going to eat it. But he certainly would fight for it.

Out of nowhere they attacked him. It was two on one this time, and Teddy took a hard blow to the head that left him with a gigantic black eye, but the home-boyz who rushed him ended up with worse. One was carried away with a nose that looked as if it had been hit with a brick. The other would be dragging his left arm for a month; Teddy had snapped his clavicle like a dry twig.

Teddy got two more days in SHU for fighting. His first night was plagued by the sound of screams from a fifteen-year-old who was trying scrape his right ear off of his head by rubbing it up against the concrete. "Special" kids in HJH always posed problems for the night shift, especially when they started hurting themselves in the dark.

The policy of SHU, however, was to try to keep kids out of the isolation units, so on the morning of day three, a man in blue jeans and a tan button-down shirt showed up at Teddy's cell. "Is it quashed?" he asked, trying to determine whether Teddy could be trusted to return to general pop.

"Is by me," Teddy responded. His beefs with these other kids weren't personal, and if they left him alone, Teddy saw no need to break anyone else's teeth.

"Then let it rest," said the man as he unlocked Teddy's cell, then escorted him back to the main unit.

There was no way for Teddy to know if he would be confronted again. There were more than two hundred different gangs represented in HJH and none of them could be counted on to behave predictably. Two weeks in juvenile jail was a very long time, and for Teddy, every minute crawled by. Forced to remain vigilant against sudden attack, Teddy remained on high alert even when things seemed calm. Kids on Killer's

Lane were capable of almost any atrocity, and it was easy to get caught off guard, especially when HJH remained filled to capacity—which was all the time. The supply of felonious juveniles in Los Angeles never ran dry.

Two weeks in HJH—it was a long time.

7

The sheer volume of criminal cases and the over-crowded prisons meant that deal-making was pretty much the only way the juvenile justice system could function; so when Teddy was pulled out of the Cage and into the hall to confer with Bill, his lawyer, two weeks later, he expected to hear an offer. Only, he had no idea what it would be.

"None of the people you have been accused of assaulting are willing to testify against you—no one wants to be a snitch—so we have the DA over a barrel on that one. However, the possession and concealed weapons charges are pretty tough to beat, and the DA is going to enhance their prosecution by tagging a gang charge on it. Your eye okay?" Bill asked.

The swelling had gone down, but there was still a trail of red blood in the white of Teddy's left eye, and his vision was still a bit blurred from his fight in the cafeteria fourteen days prior. "I'm fine. What's it all mean?"

"I think we can get you a deal for no jail time," Bill began.

On the outside, Teddy didn't show a hint of emotion, but on the inside, he felt relief. Juvenile Hall was the worst experience he'd ever had. There was no glamour. There was no romance. There was nothing cool or brave or heroic about doing time there. Places like HJH were nothing more than torture palaces for young people, and the best advice Teddy could ever give to any kid about Juvenile Hall would be, *Never go in, because you'll never be the same after you come out.*

"However," continued Bill, interrupting Teddy's thoughts, "the P.O. will only agree to this with an enhanced G-PIP probation."

"Fine," Teddy answered, not even knowing what he was agreeing to.

"Don't you want to know what that means?"

"What's the difference?" he replied. Teddy was a master chess player, who knew that sometimes over the course of a game, a player is forced into making hard sacrifices, even if he doesn't want to. After two weeks in the KL unit, Teddy knew that he was out of options.

"Just know, they are not screwing around," Bill added. "And the truth is, there is no guarantee Judge Lynch is going to accept this arrangement. Sometimes he gets a bug up his butt when it comes to gang and gun charges, and if we try to go for this, he might override our suggestion and give you jail time anyway."

"He can do that?"

"He can do almost anything he wants."

Teddy paused. "Should I go to trial and fight?" he asked.

"If we lose, he'll most likely max you out."

Teddy quickly did the calculations. He thought about the kid doing fifty-four years, plus another fifty-four right behind that. Judge Lynch was no one to mess with, that was for sure.

"Go for the deal," Teddy said.

Bill turned, then walked Teddy back into court.

"After the reports I read, you want me to agree to an enhanced probation for this young man? Do I look like a clown to you, counselor?" Judge Lynch barked. "Instinct tells me this child needs some momma time."

"Your honor, if I may add," interrupted an unidentified woman sitting in the probation officer's chair, where the short-sleeved gentleman had sat two weeks earlier. "The enhanced probation will be under the aegis of the G-PIP program."

"They got funding for that?" Judge Lynch asked. Judges and probation officers were on the same team, and a P.O.'s words often held great weight in juvenile court.

"A small amount, sir. A review of the files indicates that Mr. Anderson will make a strong candidate."

Judge Lynch looked over some notes and read the data. "Why, just because he's got some brains in his head? If he's such a damn genius, how come he's standing in my courtroom?"

"Officer Diaz is under the impression that he would—"

"Officer Diaz is going to run G-PIP?" asked the judge. After taking a moment to digest this new information, the judge turned to Teddy with a twisted smile on his face. "Oh, you're gonna like Officer Diaz. Okay, I'll play along." The judge scribbled his signature across three sheets of paper.

"But let me be very clear about something," Judge Lynch said, pointing his pen at Teddy. "I'd like nothing more than to roast you on an open barbecue as an example to all the other young punks out there who think that gangs are cool and fun and that revenge is something to take into their own hands. You wanna be a homeboy, you'd better know that there are mean old men like me out here in the courts waiting for you, and if you cross my path, I'm gonna send you to the blackest place you can imagine."

Bill was tempted to interject and point out that Teddy wasn't actually a gang member, but he held his tongue. Almost any teen arrested with a gun was likely to be enhanced with 186.22. Everyone knew that that was the DAs' way of proving they were tough on crime so that they could keep their options open to run for political office one day in the future.

Judge Lynch signed another form. "And, son, if I ever see you back in this court, even for a jaywalking ticket, I will toss you. Do you know what I mean when I say I will toss you?"

"Yeah," Teddy replied.

"'Yeah'?" Judge Lynch shouted back. "Is that how you talk to me?"

"Yes, sir," Teddy replied.

"I'm not just talking jail time, I'm talking Tehachapi time," the judge snarled. "If you thought where you were was tough, just wait until you get a look at the juvenile compound at the Tehachapi prison. Let me tell you, son, it's hell on earth."

Teddy looked at Bill, who lowered his eyes. Apparently, the word *Tehachapi* was the worst thing a juvenile could ever hope to hear.

"Make good decisions, Mr. Anderson, because if you see me again, you'll be happier to see Satan himself."

8

The ride home felt tense and strained. Teddy and Pops rode along in supercharged silence. The white of Teddy's left eyeball was scratched, his clothes were filthy, and he had probably lost eight pounds in two weeks. All in all, he looked like street scum. Eighteen city blocks passed before Pops finally opened his mouth to speak.

"Is this how I raised you?" Teddy didn't answer. "What, you were gonna get some payback? You call missing your sister's funeral payback?"

Teddy stared out the car window, not offering a response. What could he really say?

The Andersons couldn't wait for Teddy's release to hold Tina's funeral. They needed to get her body in the ground and lay her soul to rest, particularly for the sake of Mrs. Anderson. Asking Teddy's mom to wait an additional two weeks for her daughter's burial, while her son faced attempted murder charges and remained locked in jail, was simply asking too much. Bill, Teddy's lawyer, had sought a sheriff's day pass so

Teddy could go to the funeral, but Judge Lynch wouldn't hear one more word on the matter. So the funeral went on without Teddy.

"For a boy so smart, how stupid are you?" asked Pops. "I mean, holy Jesus, Teddy, you blew chemicals into a boy's face."

Teddy still didn't respond. Nor did he show a hint of regret. No matter what his father said, Teddy would never believe that those homeboyz by the liquor mart were the victims. They were perpetrators, the people responsible for murdering his sister, and one day, regardless of who tried to stop him, Teddy knew he would make them pay.

He would make them *all* pay.

Teddy still had to work out a new plan, but one day, Teddy knew, they'd meet again. He would make sure of that. And the next time he wouldn't be so nice.

Pops struggled between rage at his son and memories of the time he had gone to jail in his own quest to seek revenge for a crime that had been committed against him.

"You know, I didn't lose the hearing in my right ear falling off of no ladder."

"Yeah, I know, you got jumped by some redneck white boys in a bathroom. Save your breath, Pops. Andre told me all about it."

Pops slammed on the brakes and pulled the car off to the side of the road. "Have you lost your hot-damned mind?"

"Look, shit's changed, Pops. Changed big-time. You don't know how it is nowadays on the streets. There's no law anymore. A man's gotta take matters into his own hands."

"Oh, you a man now?"

"Well, somebody has to be."

Pops raised his hand to strike his son. Up until that moment, he had never hit any of his four children, never even came close. Pops wanted to slap his son across the mouth, give him a backhand shot that would cause his lip to bleed, let him taste some salty, red pain. But if he did that, Pops knew he'd instantly regret it. How could slapping Teddy help? Real men didn't hit their kids, Pops believed, they raised them.

Pops lowered his hand. "For all your brains," he finally said, "you have no idea what it means to be a real man."

"Well, I sure as hell know not to count on the police to make things right."

"They caught you, didn't they?" Pops said.

"So what?" Teddy fired back. "It's less than three weeks later and I'm back on the streets. Courts in this country don't work."

"The courts don't work, huh? After what you just been through you're gonna sit here and tell me that the courts in this country don't work?"

"Damn right. Gangstas don't fear the law. It's just part of a game to them. The only thing they fear, the only thing they understand, is vengeance."

"And what about you, Teddy?" Pops asked, looking at his son's ragged condition. "How do you feel about the law?"

Teddy turned his head and stared out at the street. He paused before answering. "There's a higher law," he replied. "A higher law."

Pops didn't respond, he just stared at his son in disbelief, wondering when turning into a vigilante had become the only way a young black man in this society would feel that justice had been served.

A horn honked. The rear of Pops's vehicle had been sticking out into traffic and cars wanted to pass. Pops put the car in gear and started to drive. They continued for three more blocks without another word.

"You know they got him, right?" Pops finally said. Teddy looked up. He did not know. "That's right, they got him. The law, which you do not think exists, stepped in and did its job. Caught a thug named Maggot. Arrested two nights after you, and booked as an adult on double homicide. No juvee for him. He's looking at the big house."

Teddy raised his eyes, and processed the news. He revealed no emotion.

"So what's you plan now, Mr. Genius? Get yourself arrested again, sent away for years and years to a federal penitentiary just to find this punk in jail and get a 'man's' revenge?" Teddy didn't answer. "You had a chance to go to Maryland, Teddy. A chance to participate in one of the most advanced computer programs in the country. All expenses paid."

"Whoever said I wanted to be some government cyber-spy anyway?"

"Well, don't seem like that matters much now," Pops replied, pulling into their driveway. "Seeing that the National Security Agency probably doesn't accept people with violent criminal records into their program anyway."

"Screw the NSA," Teddy answered.

"You had a chance to become one of the youngest people ever accepted into their program and now . . . Now, you're . . ." Pops stopped in midsentence, looking at his son. "You know, all that anger you got ragin' inside of you, it's only gonna end up burning yourself, Teddy. At the end of the day, it's just gonna end up burnin' you up."

Teddy didn't answer. Pops put the car in park and turned off the engine.

"Just remember, ain't no such thing as revenge, son. I've said it before and I'll say it again, there ain't no such thing as revenge." Pops opened his door and made his way toward the house. "Think you a man . . . *Hmmft!*," he added with disgust before walking inside. "Boy, you got a lot to learn."

The door closed. Teddy remained alone in the car, trying to stop his father's words from dancing through his head. Two minutes later, he decided to go inside.

Teddy's mother, brother, and sister sat silently in the living room, waiting for him. Though the burial had been many days before, their home still felt like a funeral parlor.

Teddy's scruffy, beat-up condition shocked Tee-Ay and Andre, but they both knew it wasn't their place to speak yet. They waited for their mom to break the silence.

It took her a moment. A full fifteen seconds passed before she rose from her chair and approached Teddy. Then she stepped close so she could look her son in the eye.

At first, Teddy wouldn't raise his face to meet his mother's. He couldn't stand the heat of her glare. Then he lifted his gaze and looked into her eyes. He saw a distant, empty stare. Yes, it was his mother, but she wasn't all there.

A long moment passed. Then, without a word, Mrs. Anderson broke off eye contact, lowered her head, and walked into her bedroom, closing the door behind her without a peep.

And she didn't come back out.

Teddy would have preferred she had slapped him. Or screamed. Or stuck a knife into his chest—something. *But not a word?*

Her silence hurt worst of all.

9

"Name?" asked an overweight guard on a stool. His gray T-shirt read HAWKINS MIDDLE SCHOOL: SECURITY.

Teddy looked up at the steel gate. High schools had long ago required iron fences and men with handcuffs to sit at their entrances and protect the nation's children from the ills of gangs, guns, and drugs. Urban middle schools now had them, too. "Anderson," Teddy replied.

The security guard found Teddy's name on a list, handed him a visitor's pass, and pointed him in the direction he needed to walk.

Though he hadn't attended Hawkins Middle— Teddy had gone to Winston Middle, about fifteen minutes away—he knew the layout very well. Classrooms would have colorful projects stapled around the room, but if Teddy looked closely, he would easily be able to see the cracks in the walls and ceilings. Thirty-eight desks would be arranged in rows, like soldiers on parade, facing the teacher's desk at the front; but sometimes there still wouldn't be enough chairs to accommodate all the kids. Fifty percent of the teachers would be white, and they would commute in from other communities. Hardly any white kids ever enrolled in these schools. The bathrooms would face an unending war against graffiti, the cafeterias would smell like steamed sweat socks, and the locker rooms would remain a terrifying place for any kid who wasn't popular.

Yes, it was a different school from the one Teddy had attended, he thought as he cruised through the halls, but urban middle schools were all too similar.

"Eat balls, ya melon-headed bumble ass!" an African American girl shouted to a boy as she screeched down the hall.

Oh, yeah, Teddy remembered, middle school was also when hormones began to rage and kids started to seriously curse.

After a left turn past the teachers' lounge, Teddy arrived at the door he'd been looking for: CAMPUS PROBATION OFFICER. Virtually all inner-city middle schools had such an office nowadays. Some of them saw more action than the campus library. Teddy knocked.

"Come in, I'll be with you in a second."

Teddy entered, closed the door, and scanned the

room. The office was neatly organized, with files on one side and reference materials on the other. A tan, rectangular table sat in the middle of the room, clean and free of scratches and graffiti, while photos of students in graduation robes, kids holding trophies, and fire-camp training brochures speckled the walls. The office looked nothing like what Teddy had expected for a probation officer. It was the first room Teddy had encountered in his entire journey through the juvenile justice system that reflected any positive spirit at all.

Officer Mariana Diaz appeared from an office in the back, a sort of room within a room for her use only. She too, was not what Teddy expected. "Welcome," she said.

Diaz was young, in her mid to late twenties, and pretty. She wore her hair tied back and her sweater tight. It fit her curves nicely. Teddy looked up. She had attractive Latina eyes.

"You must be Dixon," she continued.

"Teddy," he responded.

"We don't use street names in here."

"It's not my street name," he answered.

Diaz, a quizzical look on her face, peered down at the form she held. It read, "Dixon Theodore Anderson."

Teddy filled in the blanks. "Theodore became

Teddy. Before I was even born. It's what everyone has always called me."

"Teddy, huh? All right, that doesn't seem unreasonable. Have a seat."

Teddy took a chair, and while Diaz read from his file, Teddy read from the room, drawing a psychological profile of her based on all that he saw.

With her hair pulled back, Diaz gave the impression of strength and confidence, but her surroundings revealed much more to Teddy's keen eyes. Not an item was out of place. She wore no wedding band, and her nails were well manicured. Furthermore, a rain forest–fragrance room freshener was mounted on the far wall, and a box of peppermint tea rested on the counter next to a coffeemaker with no brown stains in the pot, indicating that Diaz only used the machine to boil water. Teddy quickly concluded that she liked neatness, fresh scents, and taking good care of herself, as he could tell from her kicking body.

And women who took good care of their own bodies appreciated men who had hot bodies themselves. Teddy was built like a Greek god. With his bad-boy attitude and washboard stomach, the girlies had been throwing themselves at him for years.

Teddy relaxed. *Just like I thought*, he told himself, *the courts are a freakin' joke.*

"Do you know why you are here?" Diaz inquired.

"*Mm-hmm,*" Teddy answered.

"Do you have any idea of what I expect of you?"

"I dunno, maybe you're gonna make me be a hall monitor or something."

Diaz paused, then cracked a smile. She had pretty, white teeth. "No," she said, "you are not going to be a middle-school hall monitor."

"Then how about," he suggested, "one of those dudes who stands out front after school, wears an orange vest and, you know, holds up a stop sign for children's safety."

"You mean a crossing guard?"

"Yeah, a crossing guard. I'll stop traffic for a couple of weeks, make sure all the little homies don't forget their lunch boxes, and the next thing you know, probation over."

Diaz smiled again. "Probation over?"

Teddy smiled back. "Yeah, probation over."

Teddy held his eye contact with Diaz for an extra second. After a moment, Diaz grinned a third time, a small dimple appearing on her left cheek. She certainly was cute.

"Are you flirting with me, Teddy?" she asked.

Teddy leaned back in his chair. "I don't know, Officer Diaz. I mean, I am seventeen years old.

Biologically speaking, that would put me right about at my sexual prime."

Diaz paused, then took off her glasses, placed them carefully down on the desk in front of her, and leaned forward. "Teddy," she began. Her eyes were even prettier without glasses. "You copped a plea to attempted homicide while carrying an unregistered firearm in the pursuit of gang-related activities, and now you owe our state three hundred hours of G-PIP community service. Judge Lynch sent you to me with what we informally call a *sez-me*. A *sez-me* means that if you do not do exactly as I say, exactly as I wish, all I have to do is fill out this sheet of paper, and you will find yourself back in front of the judge—*says me*."

Diaz held up a form in front of Teddy's face. His name had already been typed across the top.

"Essentially, my signature is the only thing separating you from doing eight years in a penal institution set aside for our state's most violent youth offenders, where prisoners are routinely locked down in their cells for twenty-two hours a day and permitted only two showers a week. It is a place from which there is no escape, the chances of sexual assault against you are very high, and even the most hardened criminals find themselves weeping at some point. So get this, Teddy, and get it good. I am your last chance. That means, stop looking at my breasts and absorb this message in its entirety: I own you." Diaz paused for effect. "And if you fuck with me, I'll ship you off to prison without blinking an eye."

Teddy sat motionless in his chair.

"Now, do you have anything smart-ass to say in response to the information I have just given you?"

Diaz waited for an answer, ready to write Teddy up for violating his parole right then and there. Wisely, Teddy said nothing.

Diaz reached for her glasses, put them back on her face, and smiled again with her pretty, white teeth. "Good, now that we're all clear, please follow me."

After picking up her pencil, Diaz led Teddy into the other room, to her smaller, though just as neat, office in the back.

Teddy's eyes instinctively scouted around. Three college degrees framed in dark brown wood hung on the wall. Diaz held an undergraduate degree in psychology, having graduated *summa cum laude*—with highest honors; a master's degree in criminology; and another master's in social work. Additionally, four citations from the probation department for meritorious achievement hung on the wall. There were three plants, a stuffed panda holding a sign that said SOMETIMES YOU JUST GOTTA LOOK ON THE BRIGHT SIDE, and a series of photographs in a kaleidoscope frame. Teddy gazed more closely at the pictures. He spied a photo of Diaz and two girlfriends laughing in a restaurant, a shot of her face-to-face with a horse on a ranch somewhere, a head shot of a strong-willed Latino teen with the words IN LOVING MEMORY . . . written underneath, along with another photo that appeared to have been taken many years before, when Diaz had long, straight hair and braces on her teeth. She was wearing a cap and gown.

"Sit," she instructed.

Teddy did as he was told. As he settled into his chair, Teddy observed a gold badge, a pair of handcuffs, a canister of Mace, and a cell phone sitting next to Diaz's computer.

She clicked the mouse to open some computer files. Teddy's eyes scanned back to the picture of Diaz as a young girl. It had to be her eighth-grade graduation picture—and it had been taken right on the campus of where they were now, Hawkins Middle School.

Teddy pieced together the rest of the puzzle. Diaz was an alumna of Hawkins Middle School, and underneath her youth and prettiness, she was a hometown-hero type, a girl who had gotten out of the 'hood without getting pregnant, falling victim to drugs, or dropping out of school, and had made a success of herself. And she'd come back to her community to make positive change.

The girls at the restaurant were most likely friends, possibly sisters or cousins. The horse, a photo in lieu of any sort of lovey-dovey boyfriend snapshot. Workaholics like Diaz always struggled to hold down personal relationships. The guy in the IN LOVING MEMORY . . . photo, a picture of someone who Diaz once loved—and lost—possibly a victim to the streets.

Teddy instantly realized the depth of Diaz's commitment to her job. People like her were not to be messed with. She was driven, ambitious, and looking for revenge in her own way against the unlawful elements in society that had obviously hurt her deeply. Pain was her motivation, and despite what the outer room looked like, the inner room told her real story: Diaz meant serious business and she would ship Teddy's butt off to jail in a heartbeat if he pushed it too far. Teddy shifted in his chair to get more comfortable, knowing he had no option other than to play it cool and keep the smart-ass comments to himself. Diaz was dangerous, like a snake ready to strike.

"You see, Teddy," Diaz started, "I know all about you." She clicked the mouse and brought up an online profile of Teddy.

"'Dixon Theodore Anderson . . .'" she began reading. "'High level of intelligence. Outstanding athlete but considered uncoachable. A penchant for mischief and misbehavior.'" She looked up from her files and smiled. "Wow, a troublemaker with brains and muscles. Gee, Teddy, the ladies must just love you, huh?"

Teddy stared straight ahead but didn't answer. Diaz was teasing him, and he didn't like it.

"But look at those grades," she continued. "Never really been challenged by your teachers, have you? Heck, you're probably smarter than they are anyway, aren't you, Teddy?"

He remained silent.

"You had your last tetanus shot in tenth grade, a cavity filled in ninth, and eighty-four dollars and twelve cents in school library fines were mysteriously wiped clear of your record last August. *Hmmm*, now, if I were a suspicious person, I might suspect that someone had hacked into the computer system and secretly deleted those fines. You're not aware of anyone who likes to hack, are you, Teddy?"

Teddy still didn't say a word, but inside he was becoming agitated. Everything Diaz had said was correct. How did she know so much? he wondered.

"That's right, I know it all. Now that we've

upgraded the school district's information technology systems to interface with the department of justice's records, we know more than ever about the youth of our city. It's called CLETS—the California Law Enforcement Technology System—and it's our newest weapon in the fight against youth crime."

Diaz paused and stared at Teddy. "Oh, I know what you're thinking. . . . But don't bother. It's completely hackproof. Cutting-edge software engineers have put together the most advanced firewalls and encryption our state has ever seen. Truly, you'd have better luck breaking into the computers at the Department of Social Security."

Teddy didn't answer.

"Oooh, and look at this," Diaz continued as she read more from Teddy's profile, "you missed your sister's funeral while you were in lockup." She slowly turned and looked Teddy in the eye. "How does that make you feel, Teddy? I mean, how does it make you really feel?"

Teddy glanced back to the psychology degree hanging on the wall and remained quiet, though a flash of hate crossed his eyes. Teddy burned, but he didn't say a word.

Diaz smiled. "As I said, Teddy, we know more than we ever have. Truth is, it's the reason you're here. I, for one, happen to think it'd be a shame to waste your talents by caging you for the next eight years. That's why I had Judge Lynch send you to me."

"What do you want?" Teddy asked, with an edge in his voice.

"We're going to do a gang intervention with you."

"I don't need a gang intervention."

"Not for you. *With* you. You're going to step in and help someone else."

Teddy, as Officer Diaz went on to explain, stood out as an ideal candidate for G-PIP, the Gang Prevention Intervention Program, a pilot program the county department of juvenile corrections had been trying to launch for years. The basic idea was to take the wisdom and experience of older teens caught in a web of trouble and channel their abilities and energy in a positive direction by mandating that they spend their court-ordered community service hours working as a mentor/big brother to an "at-risk" preteen.

"I ain't gonna be no role model," Teddy said after hearing Diaz's explanation of the program.

"Actually, I've got a few sheets of paper that say you are. And if you get any funny ideas about breaking the conditions of your parole . . ."

Diaz glanced at Teddy's left leg. Under his jeans he was wearing an electronic ankle bracelet. She knew this because she was the one who had ordered it placed there.

"I've chosen enhanced supervision for you, Teddy. Twenty-four hours a day, seven days a week, holidays, birthdays, and Christmas."

"How am I supposed to shower?"

"You're smart. I'm sure you'll figure it out."

Teddy was starting to see why Judge Lynch liked Diaz so much—because he knew Teddy would hate her.

"Get used to it, Teddy. You may be out of those fancy orange clothes, but the state still owns you." Diaz logged off her computer. "And let me repeat, don't even think about hacking into this system. You take even one glimpse at the operational workings of the machinery behind the scenes, and this system will know about it. You'll have violated your parole, and I'll send you straight to jail. Got me?"

No answer.

"Oh, I know you think that this might be some sort of personal challenge to prove how brilliant you are, but the whole thing will be over before it starts if you do one bit of hacking, Teddy. And trust me, people are already on the lookout for you. The computer itself is on the lookout for you. If anyone tries to go in via any way other than through the front door, the most advanced alarm ever built on the Internet will go off, and you'll be busted. I don't know all the technical terms to describe it, but I've been told by some very sophisticated engineers that you'd have a better chance of breaking into the credit card database of PayPal than you would of hacking into CLETS, so take my warning seriously, Teddy—don't even try."

"Any other rules I should know about?" Teddy asked with an obvious distaste for everything he was hearing.

"Just one. If he don't make it, neither do you."

"If who don't make it?" Teddy asked.

"Glad you asked. Follow me."

"Micah, this is Teddy, the guy I told you about."

Micah scowled. Though he stood four foot eleven, weighed 105 pounds, and was only twelve years old, Micah clearly thought of himself as a tough, seasoned warrior of the streets. "Teddy?" he asked, looking, with a gangsta's glare, up, down, and over the guy who had entered with Officer Diaz. "Thought you said da' fool's name was Dixon."

"Just call me Teddy."

"What—ya don't like the name Dixon? How 'bout if I jus' call ya Dick fo' short?" Teddy glowered.

"Whassa matter? You don't like that neither . . . Dick?"

"Call me that again and I'll rip the gums out of your mouth."

"Bring it on, mo'fo', I ain't scared a you."

Micah threw back his chair and stood up. Never mind that Micah was a foot smaller, five years younger, and a hundred pounds lighter, the kid showed no fear.

Diaz stepped between them. "All right, all right, first official meeting is Monday at one thirty. This was just a nice 'get acquainted' session. I'll see you both in my office then."

"I'm through?" asked Micah.

"Yes, you're through," she answered.

Micah grabbed his sweatshirt and headed for the door. "Peace out, Dee-az."

"Try to stay out of trouble, Micah."

"Aw, I don't look fo' trouble, Officer Dee, trouble looks fo' me." Micah smiled with a devilish grin. "Peace out . . . Dick!" Micah added as he swaggered out the door.

Teddy glared at Micah as the kid exited, then turned to Diaz. "You let him talk like that?"

"I only wish profanity were his biggest problem," she replied, locking the door to her office so she could walk Teddy to the front gate of the school. "So here's how it will work. Since it's your senior year, we've arranged for Home Studies, then you'll come to this campus at one thirty to—"

"Whoa, whoa, Home Studies?" Teddy interrupted. "You're unenrolling me in high school?"

"It's safer this way. Word is, some of the gang-bangers you messed with want payback."

Teddy's eyes turned to ice. "I can take care of myself."

"Besides, you're smart enough to earn a diploma in less than three weeks."

"I said," Teddy repeated, "I can take care of myself."

"This is *not* a negotiation, Teddy. What I say goes. Your old high school is a hornet's nest of gang activity, so in the interest of safety—both your own and that of the other kids, because goodness knows what other sick things you might cook up—I am placing you under house arrest, with permission to come here only Monday through Thursday for a couple of hours to work with Micah. That's it."

Teddy stared at her defiantly.

"And if I were you, Mr. I Can Take Care of Myself," Diaz continued, "I'd spend less time thinking of ways to argue with me and more time figuring out how to explain to your parents that they need to lock every door and be suspicious of every mysterious car that creeps down their street after nightfall. You go hunting gangsters, Mr. Tough Guy, you gotta know, they'll come hunting you."

The school bell rang, sending thousands of middle-school kids pouring out through the doors of their classrooms. Across the yard, through a crowd of students, Teddy spotted Micah. "You're kiddin' about that little fool, right?" Teddy asked.

"Not at all. He's already been pulled from his special education classes, where he's been failing terribly. You'll do all your work together in my office."

Diaz handed Teddy a file. Across the front of the folder was the boy's name, MICAH MATTHEW WHITEHALL, A.K.A. LI'L STOOP.

Teddy looked down at the folder, then back at Micah—just as Micah spotted Teddy. A moment passed, then Micah grabbed his crotch, stuck out his tongue, and flipped Teddy off with his middle finger. Teddy looked at Diaz. She saw all of Micah's actions but said nothing. Micah smiled from ear to ear, flipped Teddy a middle finger once again, then strutted off.

"You'll want to read that file from cover to cover," Diaz said.

"This is bullshit," Teddy replied.

Diaz grinned. "Your ankle bracelet means you can only come here from home, then go back home again. If all goes well for the first sixty days, I'll consider allowing you a dinner out with your family."

"Wow, you're so generous," Teddy answered.

"Just remember, Teddy. If he fails, my program fails. And if my program fails, you fail. We're like dominoes, and the last one ends in Tehachapi."

Pops's car horn pierced the air. Teddy's parole stipulated he wasn't allowed to drive, and Diaz felt that allowing Teddy to take the bus to and from Hawkins Middle would be too dangerous, since the bus route crossed right through enemy territory. So Pops was forced to make time both to drop Teddy off and to pick him up again, all according to the schedule that Diaz had set. Never mind the impact on Pops's business.

"See you at one thirty on Monday," Diaz said as Teddy approached his father's car. "And stay safe. Sometimes these gangsters are nothing but talk, but other times . . ."

Teddy climbed into his father's car and closed the door. There was no *Hello*. There was no *How was it?* There was no *Are you all right?* Without a word, Pops drove his son home.

10

When Teddy walked through the front door, he received daggerlike glares from Tee-Ay and Andre. Worse, though, was Teddy's mom. She simply stayed shut inside her bedroom.

Three months earlier, Mrs. Anderson had been like a barn on fire. She had just been promoted to senior manager, overseeing trust accounts at the bank where she worked; her oldest son was embarking on a promising career in journalism; her eldest daughter was earning fantastic grades in college; her "moody" son had just been recruited by an elite federal agency to work in computer encryption technology; and her youngest daughter, always an angel, had just taken home her third major academic trophy in two years. Life was very good.

Now her world was shattered and Mrs. Anderson had closed herself off behind her bedroom door, leaving Pops to do his best to keep both the family and the household running.

Teddy put his keys on the table. He didn't talk to

anyone and no one talked to him. *Screw 'em if they don't want me here,* Teddy said to himself. *I'm under house arrest, and home is where the courts have ordered me to be. Let them leave if they don't want to be around me. I have to stay.*

Teddy went to the kitchen to grab a glass of grape juice, but there wasn't any, so he settled for water. When he returned to the living room he paused, aware for the first time of how much Tina's death had devastated his family. Tee-Ay was snippy, Andre was sullen, Mrs. Anderson was despondent, and Pops was joyless. The pain of losing the baby of the family to gang warfare wasn't about to go away anytime soon. Nobody could just "move on." The flood of media attention and condolences from friends and neighbors had receded, but the hurt of Tina's murder had not passed.

Teddy attempted to look at the situation with a cold, dispassionate eye. Tina was dead and she was never coming back. Now every member of the Anderson household had to figure out a way to go forward with their own lives. Time would roll forward cruelly, one second, one minute, one hour, one day at a time. His family's grief would take years to mend.

Teddy gulped down the last of his water and carelessly tossed Micah's folder on the table. He hadn't read a word of it. There were other things to do, like get on his computer.

It had been weeks since Teddy had been able to do some tappin' at the keyboard, and he itched for his computer the way an addict itches for a needle. But not yet, Teddy thought. He knew he had to be patient. Pops and his siblings had their eyes on him. The last thing the Andersons wanted was to see Teddy, fresh out of jail, immediately go back to his online world of isolation, mystery, and covert maneuverings. *Just chill,* Teddy told himself. *Soon enough they'll all be in bed and you'll get your chance.*

In some ways Teddy was a freak. While other people needed at least six or seven hours of sleep each night, Teddy could live on only an hour or two for days, even weeks on end. Computers and the Internet suited his insomnia perfectly.

Teddy returned to the refrigerator to get something to eat. Usually there'd be all sorts of goodies, plenty of leftovers and snacks to munch, but not anymore. The fridge was strikingly bare.

Teddy grabbed a box of cereal and a half gallon of milk that had expired the day before and made himself an early dinner. Froot Loops were like filet mignon after the food he'd been served in HJH.

* * *

At one o'clock in the morning, with everyone else in bed, Teddy booted up his computer. "Hackproof, huh?"

Teddy began to poke around, careful not to touch anything that might set off the CLETS internal security alarms. Diaz was correct. Just a few gentle probes revealed excellent defenses against anyone without permission to access the system.

Sure, Teddy could have tried a variety of strategies in his bag of devious hacking tricks. He could have attempted to dismantle a section of the IDS—the Intrusion Detection System—and set up an intricate access loop-around. He fantasized briefly about simply brute-forcing an access password—writing a program that would try every possible combination of characters, one after another—but his machine just wasn't powerful enough. He would have needed access to servers as big as the ones at the National Security Administration to do cool things like that.

But why bother? Teddy asked himself. Why spend hours and hours trying to fight his way through the back door when he could walk right through the front?

Teddy's supreme computer abilities together with his exceptional intelligence made him a highly dangerous cyber-criminal. He knew there was no such thing as security on the Internet. All those companies that made billions of dollars selling anti-intrusion software were merely selling illusions to their clients. Technological privacy didn't exist—and never would—because the weakest link in every computer security chain could never be fixed: the human user. People, Teddy knew, were always the softest, weakest targets.

If Teddy had a dime for every person who used their pet's name as their computer password—or a nickel for everyone who used their birth date as their ATM PIN—he could have bought a beach house in Hawaii. How about all the girls who used the word *chocolate* as their password? Most people, Teddy knew, either didn't know how to create viable passwords or didn't know how to guard them—especially older people, who had grown up in a time before the Internet had even been invented. Adults were the easiest suckers of all. Teddy set his plan and began to type:

> The fall of Troy was assured when Odysseus realized
> that the Trojan city could be taken by cunning
> instead of force. He had a wooden horse built, inside
> of which a few of the Greeks' strongest fighters hid.
> It was a bold plan and . . .

The next day Teddy called Diaz. "I need to clean out my locker." There was a pause. "What, I can't have my stuff back?" he asked. "We keep our lockers for all four years at my school, and mine's full of junk. I want it back . . . if that's okay with you."

There was another pause. "You trying to pull something on me, Teddy?"

"Ya don't believe me, call the school. I mean, there ain't nothin' illegal in there, Diaz. Just give me an hour, huh?"

"How are you going to get there?"

"My pops'll drive me."

A long silence filled the phone line.

"You get half an hour. Call me back when you're ready to go." *Click.* Teddy quickly dialed his father's cell. "Officer Diaz wants me to go clean out my school locker."

"When?" asked Pops.

"She said this afternoon, and she's only giving me a half an hour."

Pops groaned, but he shifted around his work schedule, and before Teddy knew it, he was back at his high school.

But Teddy didn't visit his locker.

There was no reason to visit his locker, because there was nothing in it. And he didn't go hunting gangstas, either. Their time would come. Instead, Teddy went straight for the jugular: right to the principal's office.

"Good afternoon, Mrs. Wellman," Teddy said.

"What do you want, young man?" Mrs. Wellman asked in a hurried, emotionless tone. Mrs. Wellman was the principal's secretary, a hard woman who didn't like paperwork, bureaucracy, or kids. Why she worked in a school was anyone's guess.

"I was hoping I could print my paper for Mr. Conklin's English class on your computer."

Mrs. Wellman eyed Teddy with suspicion. She was a thirty-three-year high-school veteran. Ever since her first day of work at the school, kids had been trying to pull bullshit on her. Over the course of the last three decades, Mrs. Wellman had seen it all. *All.*

But never this. "Use Mr. Conklin's computer."

"It's busted."

"Use the library's computer."

"They have a virus."

"Go to the computer lab."

"It's closed."

"But why *my* computer, young man?" she asked with a hard edge in her voice.

"Because, Mrs. Wellman," Teddy responded with an innocent look on his face, "you seem to be the only one around this campus who knows how to do anything."

Mrs. Wellman paused. That was true, she thought.

The school was filled with idiots. "Give me your disc," she said.

The programmers who had designed the security for CLETS had done a phenomenal job. Their intrusion-detection systems were some of the finest Teddy had ever seen, with elite online burglar alarms hidden in every corner. Who knew if even Teddy, with hundreds and hundreds of hours of effort, would have been able to crack it? But with a bit of finesse and a touch of flattery, most people would simply hack themselves.

"What's the name of the file?" Mrs. Wellman asked as she inserted Teddy's disc into her computer.

"Trojan Horse," he replied.

Mrs. Wellman looked up.

"You know, Greek mythology stuff," Teddy replied quickly.

"Oh, right," she answered, double-clicking the file. Her machine started to hum.

Mrs. Wellman had no idea that Teddy was no longer a student at the school, not with 4,987 kids enrolled that year. Mrs. Wellman also had no idea that Teddy was a sophisticated cyber-thief, capable of vast and supreme deception. It wasn't as if he wore a sign around his neck identifying himself as a master hacker.

Nor did Mrs. Wellman have any idea that on this disc with his English class paper, Teddy had installed a secret key-logger program he had found on the Internet. It would capture every keystroke Mrs. Wellman entered into her own computer from that point on, and then e-mail the information back to Teddy at a free account he had set up under a false name, after routing it through a series of proxy servers in different countries. Having a key-logger program e-mail him through the chain of overseas proxy servers was like putting on a mask over a mask over yet another mask, until they were stacked so thick that it was virtually impossible to peel off the layers to find Teddy's true face underneath. Teddy also created a cyber-broom that would sweep away all traces of any electronic footprints leading from Mrs. Wellman's computer back to his, which would be crucial to his success.

The printer started to spit out Teddy's two-page paper.

The fall of Troy was assured when Odysseus realized that the Trojan city could be taken by cunning instead of force. . . .

As the principal's secretary, Mrs. Wellman was the most powerful person on campus. Principal Watkins was the kind of guy who still typed with one finger at a time, so whenever he wanted something done, Mrs. Wellman did it for him on her computer. She had access to the school's database system, attendance records, student grades, inventory and budget, and of course, to CLETS.

By midnight that night, Teddy had turned Mrs. Wellman's computer into his digital zombie, his slave. His Trojan horse had not only installed the key logger, but had enabled remote access to the secretary's machine so that Teddy could seize control of Mrs. Wellman's computer anytime he wanted. Of course, Teddy would have to be careful to do this only when she was not using it, otherwise she would immediately notice something fishy happening on her monitor. But for an insomniac like Teddy, that would be no problem at all. He did all of his hacking in the middle of the night.

Teddy set about elevating his status in the CLETS system to superuser. Then he created a series of back doors that would allow him to reenter at any time from any location undetected, and adjusted the security system to notify him in case someone probed into the inner workings of his new slave. Of course, Mrs. Wellman would never have any idea about any of this and would continue to use her computer as she always had.

Everything there was to know about any student who had ever attended any school in the district, any kid that had ever been arrested in the county, any juvenile processed through the hospitals, psych wards, nurse's stations, libraries, or bloodmobiles in the past fifteen years, now sat at Teddy's fingertips. There were academic records, police blotters, family addresses, Social Security numbers, phone contacts, district financial breakdowns, minutes of PTA board meetings—virtually everything about everything that had to do with schools and their students was available. And it was all Teddy's

It was 2:15 a.m. when he began probing the CLETS files. The first name he searched for was Tina Maryssa Anderson's.

Her online files had already been updated. In red, across Tina's latest student ID photo, was the word DECEASED. Teddy paused. His house was quiet. He scratched his leg. The ankle monitor wasn't comfortable. Then again, it wasn't meant to be.

Teddy typed another name—the one he had heard Pops mention in the car: Maggot.

Four names came up for the a.k.a., but it was easy for Teddy to find the kid he was looking for. Only one of the four had recently been arrested and charged with double homicide.

Teddy read the rap sheet on the teenager who sat in custody for killing his sister. What a monster, he thought. Wallace Stuart Christenson, a.k.a. Maggot, had been arrested eighteen times since the age of ten, with more and more serious charges on his rap sheet the older he got.

Truancy	Breaking and entering
Truancy	Assault
Narcotics possession	Narcotics possession
Truancy	Truancy
Assault	Assault
Grand theft auto	Narcotics trafficking
Assault and battery	Assault and battery
Narcotics possession	Illegal possession of a firearm
Truancy	Truancy
Truancy	Attempted murder

The more he read, the more Teddy wondered why Maggot had ever been let out of jail in the first place. This teen was a genuine menace to society, a kid they should have locked up and thrown away the key. Especially since it read at the top of his profile in big bold letters:

GANG AFFILIATE: 0-1-0
Click here to see a list of enemies

Teddy realized there would be lots more work to do that night. He had just set to work crafting a plan when Tee-Ay suddenly entered the room, wearing red pajama pants.

"Go to bed," she said.

"Kiss my ass."

"What'd you say?" Tee-Ay snapped.

"You heard me," Teddy replied, without looking up from the computer.

"You know, you got a real attitude problem."

"Eat me, I'm doing something," Teddy answered while continuing to tap away at the keyboard.

"You've got some damn nerve gettin' all mouthy with me," Tee-Ay snapped. "Especially after all the shit you've caused around this house."

"Hey, hey, keep your voices down. What're you all doin' up anyway?" Pops said as he walked in the room, rubbing the sleep from his eyes. Their father waited for an answer. Teddy's sister crossed her arms and looked to Teddy.

"I can't sleep," Teddy finally said.

"He never sleeps, Pops," Tee-Ay said. "He's been an insomniac for years now."

"Shut up, Theresa!"

"And all he does is hack into Web sites and do things he ain't supposed to do."

"Aw, so that's how it is, huh?" Teddy replied with a glare. "Now you a snitch."

"You ain't nothin' but a little punk who's bringing our whole family down, and if it was up to me—"

"Hold your tongue, Theresa, *Sshhh*. Now, Teddy, this true? You ain't been sleepin'?" Pops asked. He waited for an answer but didn't get one. "Oh, I am strugglin' with you, boy. Strugglin' hard. But if you want to talk about it, I will try to walk that road with you."

"I don't want to talk to no one, Pops. 'Specially you."

"Don't you disrespect Pops like that," Tee-Ay snapped.

"Look who's talkin'. You spent years dissin' everyone under this roof, and now that you in college you think you're all that? Well, let me tell ya something, Tee-Ay: you ain't."

"At least I got into college. What are you gonna do with your future?"

"Don't worry about my future. I'm plannin' a foot-up in it."

"What the hell is a foot-up?" Tee-Ay asked.

"It's a foot up your ass if you keep giving me grief."

Tee-Ay lunged at Teddy, who threw back his chair and stood up tall. This was not going to be the same fight it would have been when Tee-Ay lived at home. Teddy was bigger and stronger now, and by the look in his eye, it appeared that he had been waiting a long time to kick his sister's ass.

Pops struggled to hold his daughter back. Theresa showed no fear.

"Come here, you little punk!" Tee-Ay screamed. "I'll slap you into tomorrow!"

"Yo, what's going on in here?" asked Andre, entering the room.

"He's got no respect for nobody," Tee-Ay shouted, pointing at Teddy. "Especially Pops."

Andre turned and looked at Teddy, who stood at the other end of the room, flexed and ready for a fight. "What is wrong with you?" Andre asked.

"Hey, don't blame me. If he would've listened and we'd've moved out of this house like Mom had wanted to years ago, ain't none of this would have happened!" Teddy said, pointing at Pops. "Ain't my fault the shit that's goin' on around here. It's his."

Everyone stared at Pops, and the room fell silent. What Teddy said had been cold, insensitive, and ugly—but true. Years ago the Andersons had held a family conference to consider selling the house and moving out of the neighborhood because youth violence in the community had been growing out of control. Mom wanted to go. Pops wanted to stay. They ended up staying, and now Tina was dead.

Pops looked down at his brown slippers, visibly hurt by Teddy's words.

Andre saw his father's pain and moved closer to Teddy with a rare look of rage in his eyes. "You are way out of bounds."

"Yeah, and who's gonna keep me in?"

"You know, I think you're forgetting who the big brother is," Andre said. "I've been kicking your ass since you were three years old."

"Times change, bro'," replied Teddy. "You studied history, you should know that. Times change."

"They ain't changed that much," Andre answered.

Andre moved so close, the two brothers were nose-to-nose.

"Well," Teddy answered, "let's find out."

Teddy threw a punch that drilled Andre in the mouth, but Andre fired back and tagged Teddy on the chin, then tackled him over the coffee table. Though Teddy was an excellent brawler, Andre enjoyed a psychological advantage. Once a big brother, always a big brother.

Pops rushed to break up the fight, but his sons were doing everything they could to rip each other's head off.

"Kick his ass, Andre! Kick his ass!" Tee-Ay shouted.

A lamp broke. A vase smashed to the ground. Pops tried his best to get in between his boys, but he ended up getting tossed onto his back, and he crashed into the wooden leg of the couch.

"Urrgggh," he groaned.

The brothers fought fiercely, punches flying everywhere. Suddenly, everything stopped and the room fell silent.

Mrs. Anderson stood in the doorway. She looked on. Just looked. No words, no sounds, just an empty gaze in her eyes.

After another moment of watching what her family had been reduced to, Mrs. Anderson tightened the tie of her blue bathrobe, turned, and walked back into her bedroom. She closed the door behind her softly saying absolutely nothing.

Teddy's lip was bleeding. Andre's eye had started to swell. Pops struggled to his feet, a cut above his right eye with a dribble of blood running down his face. Tee-Ay looked around the room. It was a total wreck. The fight was over.

Teddy was the first to move. He stood up, straightened his chair, then sat back down at his computer and started to tap at the keyboard once again. Pops and Tee-Ay watched in disbelief. Teddy checked his bleeding lip and paid absolutely no attention to anyone else in the room.

If Pops hadn't been so cheap and had paid for another cable connection in Teddy's room, he could have worked in solitude.

Another moment passed before Andre stormed off to his bedroom. Tee-Ay threw a look of disgust at Teddy, then crossed the room to look at the cut over Pops's eye. Pops pushed his daughter's hand away and stared at his son. Teddy didn't look back, he just continued his search, a quest for all the information he could find out about Parole Officer Mariana Diaz.

"He's a lost cause, Pops," Tee-Ay said with a shake of her head. "A lost cause," she repeated, loud enough for Teddy to hear. And then she walked into her bedroom.

Teddy's eyes never left the computer screen.

||

There would be no sleep tonight, Teddy thought. It was time for people to pay.

But first, the ankle bracelet. The black electronic device strapped to Teddy's leg was irritating both his skin and his psyche. He hated the rash it caused below his calf, but more than that, he hated the sense that his freedom was being restrained. But not for long, he thought.

Teddy took a letter opener and started prying at the hinges of the device that kept him under surveillance. However, after a moment of tampering, it dawned on him that, while he could easily extract the hinge pins and free himself, taking off the ankle bracelet would automatically trigger a wireless alarm that would shoot a pager alert to Diaz, informing her that the device had been removed.

It was 2:24 a.m. Teddy had no direction, no destination, and no plan. Removing the ankle bracelet out of simple frustration, he reasoned, with nowhere to go, with no place to be, without the supplies he needed to succeed in realizing his goals, was a bad idea.

Teddy put the letter opener down and looked at the bigger picture. If he really wanted freedom, he would need a more intelligent scheme. *Don't be emotional,* Teddy told himself. *Be smart. Put together a plan.*

Teddy realized that the day's activities had left a lot of evidence on his laptop. The last thing he needed was to store incriminating information on his own hard drive. If Diaz were to have Teddy's home computer searched by some Department of Justice whiz kid seeking evidence that he had violated his parole by illegal hacking, it would be game over.

Teddy slipped a brand-new pocket-size external hard drive out from a false drawer he had built in his desk and set about transferring all of his illicit electronic files to the small device. Soon his computer was wiped clean of any trace of illegal activity, pure as virgin snow. With everything he needed on the external hard drive, which he could disconnect and hide as needed, Teddy had covered his tracks. However, as Teddy knew, it always paid to be extra safe, so he executed a whole-disc encryption on the external disc, so that even if anyone found it, the external hard drive would appear to be unformatted—completely blank.

With his own security system safely in place,

Teddy began to formulate two plans. The first was for Maggot. While there may not have been a way to attack him personally, Teddy knew he could get him using technology. With a computer, you could hurt a person. Hurt them bad.

Teddy searched the CLETS confinement catalog to locate the detention facility where Maggot was being held. A variety of options lay at his fingertips. Wicked ideas crossed through Teddy's brain, none of them cruel enough, in his opinion, to make up for the slaying of his sister Tina.

At first glance he liked the medical options best. For example, Teddy could add a mental-health condition to Maggot's official prison health records that would require the administration of powerful psychotropic drugs, turning Maggot into a brain-dead pill junkie. After a bit more research, Teddy also learned that electroshock therapy was still being administered to "treat" troubled prisoners in certain parts of California. So he could arrange to have convulsion-inducing electrodes clamped onto Maggot's head while he lay strapped on a stretcher, in leather restraints, and got zapped with electric current. Teddy knew it would be easy to manipulate Maggot's medical records, because the CLETS computer security had been designed in what's known in the security world as "M&M style." This meant that, while CLETS security was hard on the outside, it was soft and chewy in the center. Yes, it was tough to crack into, but once in, Teddy could go anywhere he wanted. CLETS was like a highway with one monster roadblock to enter, then no further checkpoints along the way. Now that Teddy was in with superuser-level security clearance, he had permission to alter any file, change any directive, or override any system command in the entire juvenile justice system. Teddy was invisible and anonymous, yet had total and complete control . . . just the way he liked it.

Unfortunately, Teddy discovered, Maggot's trial had yet to begin, so he was still being held in "transitional incarceration accommodations," which meant that he wasn't yet in a state prison, the kind that used the crude medical procedures Teddy longed to apply.

Once again, in order to be most effective, Teddy would have to be patient. But he was okay with that. Teddy was beginning to understand why, as an old saying goes, "Revenge is a dish best served cold."

In the interim Teddy could set to work on plan number two: stealing three-quarters of a million dollars in cold cash from the local school district. It would be the biggest heist in the state education system's history, and they would never know what had hit them.

Hey, if I'm going to work at Hawkins Middle, Teddy thought, I might as well get paid for it.

As he set up his scheme to swindle hundreds of thousands of dollars from the local school district, Teddy recalled how his ninth-grade science teacher had once told him that he should care about his community.

What a joke, he thought. Society didn't give a damn about him. If it did, why would it allow the schools he attended to be filled with drug dealers and gangbangers, the streets he walked to be riddled with weapons and crime, and the politicians who made all the decisions to be so corrupt?

Hacking into CLETS and poking around in the guts of the system allowed Teddy to get a firsthand look at all the bullshit that really went on in an inner-city school district—particularly with the budget. After just a little bit of investigation, Teddy discovered that almost every contractor who had ever won a bid to patch a roof, mend a fence, or paint a wall was a relative of a school board member.

Like the people who had been hired to resurface the school's running track. It turned out the company that successfully bid for the $100,000 project was managed by the brother-in-law of Dr. Bruncey, the District Superintendent. Not a bad fee, Teddy thought. Especially for a guy who owned a pet supply store.

Teddy's close examination of the available records showed that Dr. Bruncey's brother-in-law had subcontracted the job to a cut-rate outfit that had resurfaced the track at a lower price than the school had allotted for the project. Why? So he could keep the difference as profit for himself. He might have even split the windfall with Dr. Bruncey, but there would be no paper trail for such an under-the-table arrangement. At inner-city schools, it seemed that almost all construction and renovation projects were subcontracted in similarly shady ways. The records also showed that this had been the second time in seven years that the Hawkins Middle School track had been resurfaced. And Hawkins Middle School didn't even have a track team, only a track club. But when the school board district voted and all the ayes were counted, who was left to question such decisions? Nobody.

Next month they'd be voting on repaving the teachers' parking lot, and the assistant superintendent's second cousin, a dentist by trade, would be hired to oversee the next school renovation program. Its cost to Hawkins Middle: $75,000.

No wonder so many people worked so hard to

gain a seat on the local school board. The official pay was squat, but the amount of money that could be made on the side was enough to buy a four-bedroom vacation home in Palm Springs.

The more research he did, the more bitter Teddy became, because, as he knew from firsthand experience, the ones who suffered the most from all of this criminal greed were the kids. Couldn't that money have been spent on more supplies? Teddy thought. Couldn't that money have been spent on more teachers? Couldn't that money have been spent on better security?

Tina was not the first person Teddy had ever known to get blasted. Hardly. Once, Teddy had heard about a study showing that approximately forty-five percent of kids who live in the 'hood had either seen a dead body or watched a person get shot, before age fifteen. When Teddy first heard that stat, he was horrified—horrified that the number was so low. The real number was probably closer to seventy-five percent, he thought. Government studies always lie about statistics, so as not to make themselves look too bad.

Teddy's own experience had happened a few years back, and he had never told a soul about it. He was walking home with his childhood friend Marco, drinking Slurpees, when five older homeboyz—one of them looked like he was about twenty-five—rolled up on them shouting some mess at Marco about how his big brother had crossed the wrong people. Marco didn't even have a big brother. But in the 'hood, what difference did that make? Speaking reason to gangsters like this when it was five on two was just asking for more trouble. There was only one thing to do. Drop their Slurpees and run.

Both of them knew it, too. If Marco and Teddy stuck around too much longer, a severe beat-down was certain. The real problem was, Teddy knew, these homeboyz might have been strapped.

Teddy quickly devised a plan. Marco knew he could count on Teddy to come up with something brilliant to save their rear ends, so he waited for Teddy to make the first move. After a moment's eye contact with Marco, Teddy tossed his Slurpee into the face of the boy standing on his far right, creating a temporary distraction. When the homeboy stepped back, in shock at the sensation of the icy liquid hitting his face, he left an opening on his right flank, through which both Teddy and Marco could dash. Both boys were good athletes, so Teddy figured he and Marco could make it into the mall parking lot, then into one of the local department stores, before the gangstas caught up with them. And although they'd get chased, only a really sick and reckless homeboy would gun down a person in the suit section of a men's department store. They'd get caught on tape and busted for sure. Teddy knew that heading for a place of public business was the safest route. By the time he got to the men's belt section, the kids who were chasing him had given up. Teddy's plan had worked.

But Marco's plan met with disaster. For some reason Marco figured that Teddy's eye contact meant they should split up. So after the Slurpee hit the homeboy in the face, Marco raced off by himself, into the yards behind a nearby residential area. Two chased Teddy, three chased Marco.

Marco jumped a fence, then another, then another, racing through backyards. But the problem with backyards is that they are private—things can happen there that no one can see. The other problem is that some of them have really big bushes and you can get cornered easily.

Marco found himself trapped on the back lawn of Mrs. Bermuda's house. He pounded on the door. "Let me in! Please, let me in!"

Mrs. Bermuda jumped out of her chair in terrible fright and looked out the small glass window of her back door. First she saw Marco, then she saw three homeboyz jump her fence.

"Let me in! Please!"

Mrs. Bermuda reached for the lock on the back door—double-checking to make sure it was bolted tight.

"Let me in, please!" Marco pleaded.

They filled Marco's chest with five bullets in broad daylight.

The shooter then pressed his face up to the glass window of the back door and looked inside. His eyes made contact with Mrs. Bermuda's, and the homeboy made the gesture of a slit across his throat: *Say anything to anyone and we'll be back for you and your whole fucking family.*

The three homeboyz jumped back over the fence and dashed off, leaving Marco lying in a pool of red blood on the green grass.

When the police showed up, Mrs. Bermuda claimed to have been in the bathtub with the radio turned up loud the entire time. Matter of fact, she said, she hadn't known that someone was dead in her backyard until the police showed up. "Sorry, officers, can't help you with nothin'."

When Teddy got home later that afternoon, his mother asked him how his day at school had gone.

"Fine," he replied.

Teddy took a seat at his computer and pretty much

never got up again, losing all interest in school and isolating himself in an online world of solitary confinement. He still went to class, but earned only C grades. A's, he discovered, brought positive attention. F's brought negative attention. C's brought Teddy nothing but anonymity, except for the occasional "I know you can do better" from his family and teachers. For the most part, people left him alone. Just the way he wanted it.

Teddy developed a routine that had not changed since. He sat at his computer, did five hundred sit-ups a night, and worked his way through a series of self-taught martial arts moves beginning every evening at 10 p.m. until he was soaked in sweat. Then he'd shower at 11:30 p.m., eat three peanut-butter-and-banana sandwiches with the crusts cut off, which Tina had left out for him, and return once again to the computer. He only slept from 4:20 to 5:30 a.m., his mind never allowing his body any more rest than that.

The less time he spent with his eyes closed, the less chance the nightmares would come back.

Though Teddy had teased and tormented his younger sister Tina many times, she had been, in truth, the only one in the family who had understood him. No, she hadn't understood why his mood was often so dark, but while everyone else yelled at Teddy, angrily venting their frustrations with him, accusing him of failing to live up to his potential—*You're so smart and you are wasting your life and blah, blah, blah* . . . Tina had simply accepted Teddy for who he was.

Tina had seen Teddy as her big brother—the smartest, most bravest, most best-est big brother in the whole, wide world—and she'd looked up to him with nothing but love and admiration. Andre was her big brother too, but so many years separated them that they weren't nearly as close.

As Tina had grown older, her routine around the house had become fairly consistent. After she'd done her homework and chores—Tina had always been an A student and certainly bound for a great college one day—she'd tend to Teddy's needs before she went to bed. While the world cursed and screamed and challenged and raged at Teddy, Tina made her moody brother peanut-butter-and-banana sandwiches every night. They never talked about it. Tina would just leave the sandwiches on the counter the way you'd leave a bowl of milk for a stray cat on the sidewalk, and in the morning the food would be gone.

Now Tina was gone. And the gangsta who had killed her would soon be gone too.

Teddy's ever-growing thirst for vengeance made

him understand that revenge was exactly like what Pops had described it to be. The more you seek revenge, the more your whole life slips into its dark clutches. But Teddy didn't care.

Or at least, he tried not to care. He tried not to slide down into the black, bottomless pit of rage that consumed him more and more often. Yet he couldn't ignore the feeling that he was becoming a monster. He hated the fury, he hated the hate. But most of all, Teddy hated his father for being right.

Teddy glanced down at his ankle bracelet, ready to rip it from his leg and dash off into the darkness, never to be heard from again.

He hesitated. *No*, he thought, *not yet*. Teddy considered his plan. He'd pretend to be sincere. He'd pretend to care about reforming himself. He'd quietly serve his probation hours, lie low for a few months, let go of pursuing any more gangbangers, and then finish off his two-tier scheme. Part one: he'd let Maggot get sentenced by the courts, then arrange for something devastating to happen to him through the medical staff in prison. Part two: he'd scam the local school district for more than three-quarters of a million dollars. Then—*poof!* . . . Teddy would *dis-ap-pear.*

Besides, he thought, who'll really miss me any-way?

Teddy had planted the seeds of his newest scam during the Brussels Sprouts Farting Affair. That was a caper Teddy had pulled off in middle school, not long before he got himself majorly busted for hacking into his school's computer system. Essentially, Teddy had used the school district's database to send out a few thousand letters informing the students' families that the Vice President of the United States was coming to visit campus, and that he loved boiled Brussels sprouts. He'd only done it to be mischievous—to see if he could fill up the entire school auditorium with the fartlike smell of the vile vegetable. Problem was, he'd succeeded. The smell was nasty, and thousands of parents had sat in the stench for over an hour and fifteen minutes until the school's principal explained that it was only a small joke played by one of the school's students. And, oh, did Teddy get in trouble for it.

The grief he'd caught from campus administration, the interest he'd attracted from the department of cyber-intelligence at the NSA, and the hell he'd caught from his parents taught Teddy the importance of covering his hacking tracks. When he was finally allowed back on a computer, after what seemed like years to him, Teddy had dedicated himself to becoming proficient in the art of avoiding identification and detection.

At night, while his parents had been asleep and the world was at rest, Teddy spent hours and hours teaching himself how to weave intricate Internet hacks, breaching network and server security in universities, corporations, and governmental institutions all over the globe. He would route his schemes through chains of proxy servers to cover his tracks. He was always careful to select countries that had no laws against computer crime, or no resources to investigate reports of criminal activity from foreign police agencies, making it virtually impossible for his actions to be detected, much less prosecuted.

Teddy had started close to home, practicing on people who gave him grief. Once, his English teacher, Mr. Nolan, had caught Teddy reading a book about World War II code breakers instead of a classic novel by Jane Austen, and had humiliated him in front of the class, so Teddy had shifted the class of service on Mr. Nolan's home telephone number to a toll-free line and posted it on a Russian porn site.

For six weeks Mr. Nolan got calls all night long from perverts in Kiev, breathing obscenities in Ukrainian.

As he grew older, Teddy had become more

sophisticated, learning the art of leaving complicated false leads on Web sites around the world. People who tried to discover his identify would end up being led to private message boards with notes posted from Teddy written in their local language—Chinese, Korean, Finnish, whatever—saying things like "Dog poop stinks and so do you—I am UNCATCHABLE!" In a uniquely hackerish way, Teddy had also mastered the art of being annoying.

The truth was, only the FBI could catch Teddy. Since the Brussels Sprouts Farting Affair he'd become algorithmically sophisticated, borderlessly international, and utterly ruthless, a true cyber-killa.

As Teddy cruised through CLETS, analyzing the finances of Hawkins Middle, the local district, and the state school system, his confidence swelled. He knew he'd be almost impossible to capture once his scheme had been finalized and set in motion. Planning became his sole focus.

And no more Mr. Liquor Store Owners this time. I won't be stopped again.

Teddy studied the district budget numbers with a keen eye. What he needed was a pattern. The school's financial statements were almost too gigantic to comprehend. School districts, Teddy was discovering, spent a lot of money.

And they spent it on a lot of things, too. Really, who could keep track? Employee payrolls, red pens, photocopy machines, postage meters, cafeteria food, security, toilet paper, fire extinguishers, graffiti removal, yearbook photos, field trips, back-to-school night, textbooks, telephones, computer repair, report card mailings . . . the list went on and on. The budget reports Teddy examined were literally like those of a miniature city.

What is the pattern? Teddy wondered. *There's got to be a simple answer. Look for something obvious.*

Suddenly, while he was examining an invoice explaining how many sheets of yellow construction paper the district's art department had purchased for the prior three fiscal years, the key to the puzzle dawned on him: *The entire budget was all tied to one thing: attendance.* There it was, the simple answer.

Public schools were allocated their money by the State Department of Education according to how many students attended class. That was why teachers were always being warned about keeping good records. Grades, quiz scores, actual learning were all fine and dandy, but the accountants in the district and state offices would only approve the release of funds to pay a school's bills—including the bills for repaving the running track and the teachers' parking lot—

if the school kept accurate attendance records.

His plan became crystal clear. Teddy would simply add one hundred fictitious students to the school district roll sheets that were being electronically reported to the state, while keeping the true number of students exactly the same. In the old days, before the Internet, this was called keeping two sets of books, but in the modern-day world of online swindling, it was simpler than that. All that Teddy needed were two sets of computer records, one for the district, one for the state.

If the state believed there were more students attending class, they would send more money. And if the state sent more money, Teddy could reroute the cash into a secret account before anyone realized it had even been sent. All that his plan required was writing the code for the necessary hacks and creating a secret budget account.

And just in case a school bookkeeper got a sense that there was some discrepancy and wanted to examine the small deviation within the district's immense financial structure, Teddy would craft a security zone around his hack so elaborate that any accountants who wanted to gain access would first have to hire an encryption specialist to crack Teddy's digital defenses.

Teddy knew it would take months, if not years, for

his scheme to be discovered, assuming that the school ever figured it out. Teddy was dealing with a bureaucratic government organization that struggled year after year with simply getting report cards out on time. Catching an invisible cyber-thief, who had made a slave out of one of the most critical computers on one of its numerous campuses, while pilfering monies artificially inflated by altered data sent electronically to the state, would be virtually impossible.

Moreover, if someone did start to sniff around, Teddy would be reading Mrs. Wellman's e-mails. If the principal gets notified, so will I, Teddy thought with a small smile.

Using Mrs. Wellman's computer, Teddy readjusted the official Hawkins Middle School enrollment reported to the state from 3816 to 3916 students. Since the per-pupil budget for the current fiscal year stood at $7,790 for each kid, adding a hundred students would result in an additional $779,000 to be paid in monthly installments to Hawkins Middle, starting immediately. Perfect, Teddy thought.

Then Teddy set up a secret district budget account into which he could siphon off the money. As he created this account, Teddy realized he'd need to give it a fancy, school-type–sounding name for the official records. *Let's call it a "Type II Special Services" fund*, Teddy thought. *Yeah, that sounds all school-y.*

Before the evening had ended, more than three-quarters of a million dollars was scheduled to be deposited into Teddy's new "Type II Special Services" account by the last day of the current academic year. Teddy would eventually have to figure out how to transfer the funds from the Type II Special Services fund into a real-world bank account in some foreign country. But he had time for all that.

And *Poof!* Teddy—just like the money—would *dis-ap-pear*.

12

Teddy arrived on Monday afternoon at 1:23 p.m., seven minutes early, in an attempt to make a good impression on Diaz. If he had to "mentor" this little punk Micah for the next few months, he'd accept the cards he was dealt and play them out with a go-getter attitude. What did any of this G-PIP bullshit really matter? In the back of his mind, Teddy knew the dealer was in the process of a big reshuffle, and the new deck of cards would be reloaded for Teddy with nothing but aces.

Diaz had determined that the G-PIP program required a hands-off approach so that each pair of participants could determine their own relationship. While she could force Teddy and Micah to spend time together, she couldn't force them to be friends. If they were going to bond, they'd have to do it on their own.

"So what you are saying is, you don't have a plan for me?" Teddy asked.

"Just handle things the way you think they need to be handled," Diaz replied. "I'm not going to micromanage."

"And that means?"

"It means what it means, Teddy. Figure it out."
Just then Micah walked through the door.

"Hey, look who it be . . . the dick."

Teddy turned to Diaz.

"Micah," Diaz said, "his name is Teddy."

"Dick's name is Teddy? Aw, my bad, dude, my bad. How 'bout if I just call ya Dicky Tee?"

Teddy waited for Diaz to step up and say something to straighten this kid out, really snap him into shape the way she had snapped Teddy into shape when he had been a wise-ass with her the week before.

"I'll be in my office if anyone needs me," Diaz said, then left the room.

Teddy shook his head in disbelief. *If this kid says one more thing, I am gonna rip the freakin' tongue out of his— Chill, just chill, dude. Remember, you got bigger fish to fry than this little fool,* Teddy said to himself

Teddy calmly took a seat at the long, rectangular table, determined to not let this stupid little kid get the better of him.

"Aw, wassup, Dick? I'm just playin'," Micah said, enjoying his freedom to tease Teddy now with no fear of consequences. "Hey," Micah continued, looking at the bruise Teddy's fight with Andre had left on his face, "what happened to yo' lip, Dick? You get slapped by yo' mommy?"

Teddy clenched his fist. Micah grinned wide, his white teeth flashing a devious grin. In Teddy's opinion, what this kid really needed was a good ass-whipping.

Just chill, T-Bear. Just chill.

Teddy unclenched his fist and turned back to the clock on the wall. An hour and a half with this runt and no instructions on what to do was a very long time.

"You got math homework?" Teddy asked.

"Nope."

"English homework?"

"Nope."

"Social studies homework?"

"Nope."

"You got any homework at all?"

"Nope," answered Micah, puffing out his cheeks like a blowfish.

Teddy stared. Micah stared back, cold and defiant.

"What? It's da' truth, fool."

Maybe it really *was* time to kick this little kid's ass.

"Aw, whatever," Teddy said, more to himself then to Micah. Thank goodness I brought my headphones, he thought as he reached into his backpack. Teddy started pumping a beat.

Micah, without headphones of his own, looked at

Teddy with a tinge of jealousy. Then, with nothing to do other than watch Teddy nod his head up and down, grooving to the beat of a hip-hop tune he could hardly hear, Micah reached inside his backpack and took out a pad of colored construction paper and started to draw.

The two of them sat that way for what seemed like forever. Neither spoke. Diaz didn't come out and force them to do anything, and the minutes crawled by as if the second hand on the clock had been tied down with an anchor.

When the clock finally said three, the school bell rang and they left without saying good-bye. Diaz approached Teddy on his way out the door.

"How'd it go?"

"The truth? This is the stupidest program ever."

"You two just need to find your commonality."

"Me and that punk? We ain't got no commonality."

"We all have commonality, Teddy. Tomorrow. One thirty."

"Whatever you say, Officer *Deeeeee*," Teddy replied, pronouncing Diaz's name the way Micah had pronounced it.

Diaz stopped, then turned. "By the way, tomorrow . . . no headphones."

Teddy looked at his music player. *Damn.*

"Aw, you gotta learn to look on the bright side, Teddy."

"What bright side?" Teddy replied.

"That's one and a half hours down and only two hundred and ninety-eight and a half hours more to go." Diaz smiled. Teddy headed for the door. "And one more thing . . ." Diaz added before Teddy was out of the room. "Don't screw with the ankle bracelet. It's got a tamper alert."

Diaz smiled again. She knew it all.

Teddy returned the smile, a big grin on his face.

She only thinks she knows it all. Lie low, do the time, and in a few months . . . Poof! Dis-ap-pear.

"Have a nice afternoon, Teddy."

"Oh, you too, Officer Diaz. You too."

Teddy climbed into his father's car without saying hello, then put his headphones back on. A second later he reached for the volume, turned the music up extra loud, and waited for the car to take him home.

Pops glared, then pulled away from the curb as if he were Teddy's court-appointed chauffeur.

Andre walked through the living room carrying his black suitcase while Tee-Ay waited in the car, ready to drive him to the airport. Andre was going back to his job as a freelance magazine writer in Northern

California. Tee-Ay was leaving too, heading back to her on-campus apartment at the University of Southern California. It was time for both of them to return to their lives, unsettled though everything was at home.

"I'll call you when I arrive, Pops."

Andre hugged his father and looked over at Teddy, who was sitting with tools spread out across the kitchen table, adding additional memory and an accelerator card to his computer. Andre stared, waiting for his younger brother to say something.

What's he expect, a hug? Gimme a fuckin' break, Teddy thought as he plugged in his powerfully enhanced machine.

Andre continued to wait.

"Don't forget to write," Teddy finally said.

Andre shook his head, not bothering to dignify his brother's comment with a response. He grabbed his coat, picked up his bag, and headed for the door. "Like I said, I'll call, Pops."

The front door closed. After the sound of Tee-Ay's car had receded into the distance, the house fell quiet, with just Teddy and Pops in the living room. Andre was gone. Tee-Ay was gone. Tina was gone. Mrs. Anderson lay quietly in the back bedroom, gone in her own way, too.

Teddy started working again, ready to jump back online. While his plans were starting to take shape, he still had a lot of code to write.

A moment later Pops walked across the living room and ripped the computer's power cord out of the wall.

"Hey! You could of crashed my—"

Pops shoved his finger in Teddy's face. "I will never give up on you! You hear me? I will never give up!"

Teddy looked up, wondering if his father had lost his mind.

"You hear me, boy? I will *never* give up. Never! Ever! Ever! You may be smarter than me. You may be stronger than me. You may be crueler than me. But you are my son and I am your father and I love you. I've already lost one child to the streets, I will not lose another!" Pops removed his finger from Teddy's face. "Say what you want and do what you will, but know one thing, Teddy. I will never give up on you."

With that, Pops limped out of the room. He still had a hitch in his stride from the hard fall he had taken trying to break up the fight between Teddy and Andre. A moment later, the master bedroom door closed.

Teddy sat alone, the quiet ticking of the wall clock the only sound remaining.

13

The rest of the week with Micah was more of the same.

"Hey, wassup, Dick?"

Teddy rolled his eyes. "Got any math homework?"

"Nope."

"English homework?"

"Nope."

"Social studies homework?"

"Nope."

"You got any homework at all?"

"Nope," Micah said, puffing out his cheeks like a blowfish once again."

Without headphones, Teddy took out a book. Diaz couldn't really fault him for reading, could she? The title: *Notorious Hacking Crimes Revealed.* Micah doodled on his pad of colored paper.

Once during the week, Teddy had tried to sneak a peek of what Micah had been scribbling, but Micah covered up the paper with his elbow, not letting Teddy gaze into his private matters. Probably a bunch of gang crap anyway, Teddy thought. Li'l homies loved to scribble their crews' symbols anywhere they could.

The days of the first week dragged along. Each afternoon when the school bell rang at three o'clock, Teddy and Micah parted ways, not a word exchanged between them.

It took no time at all for Teddy to figure out that there was a lot at stake for Diaz in the experiment. He realized if he and Micah couldn't work together in a productive way that she could quantify statistically, the state would cut off her funding and shut her down, holding up G-PIP as just another example of how any attempt to rehabilitate gangbangers was doomed to failure.

Jail, not innovative approaches like Diaz's, was the American answer to juvenile crime. Teddy knew as well as Diaz that the United States had more people in jail than any other country in the world, both in absolute numbers and as a percentage of the total population. Millions of people were in lockup, millions more had once been in lockup, and millions more were destined to go there. *Jail 'em good and throw away the key* had become standard procedure for dealing with kids in trouble with the law—especially black- or brown-skinned kids, who were literally overloading the system, as Teddy could see from the stacks of case files piled all over Diaz's tidy office.

Diaz felt she had a better approach for the problem of youth gangs—something more humane.

However, her first experiment was clearly failing miserably.

Though Teddy desperately itched to roll the blue Honda Accord out of the garage and take it for a cruise, he knew Diaz would be alerted if he did. The ankle bracelet forced Teddy to remain within eighty feet of his home base or he would be in violation of his parole. Teddy loved technology, but he hated when it worked against him.

Fortunately, Teddy's scam of ripping off the school by altering the attendance records was working well. However, Teddy had no choice but to do his time without making waves so he could let his scheme play through on the down low. While layin' low sounded sexy when people said it in the movies, in real life, layin' low was horribly boring. There were only so many rooms in the house. There were only so many shows on TV. There were only so many hours Teddy could sit in his chair and tap away at the keyboard. And considering that Teddy hardly ever slept, house arrest for him was that much more severe a punishment. Lots of juveniles sentenced to wear ankle bracelets spent ten or eleven hours a night sleeping to kill the boredom. Teddy still never slept more than an hour and fifteen minutes each evening. Home had become a suffocating prison. His only avenue of escape was Hawkins Middle, but when Teddy showed up the following Monday, Micah simply gave him more of the same.

"Wassup, Dick?"

"Any math homework?"

"Nope."

"English homework?"

"Nope."

"Social studies homework?"

"Nope."

"You got any homework at all?"

"Nope."

Teddy took out his book, Micah doodled in his pad of colored paper, and the school bell rang after what seemed to be about seven hundred hours of torturous boredom for both of them. And of course, when they left for the day, they did so without muttering a word to one another. The pattern repeated itself on Tuesday, Wednesday, Thursday, and then on the following Monday. Micah and Teddy were both stubborn as a locked front door.

Then, on the following Tuesday, thirteen days into the program, the pattern broke.

"Wassup, Dick?"

"Any math homework?"

"Nope."

"English homework?"

"Nope."

"Social studies homework?"

"Nope."

"You got any homework at all?"

"Nope."

Teddy took out a book and Micah started doodling. Two seconds later Teddy slammed his book shut.

"So what's your deal, dude? Are you retarded?"

"Up yours, Dick."

"I told you not to call me that."

"I ain't scared a you—"

"Don't say it. I am warning you, don't say it—"

"Dick!" Micah exclaimed.

"That's it!" Teddy stood up. "You're gettin' an ass-whipping now." He grabbed Micah and put him in a headlock.

"Let me go, Dick! Let me go!"

Spying some Elmer's glue on the counter, Teddy dragged Micah over to the other side of the room.

"I'm gonna teach you the nastiest lesson you ever learned about poppin' off."

"Dick! Dick! Dick!" Micah shouted.

"All right, street rat, open up." Teddy untwisted the Elmer's top. "Time to glue your tongue to the roof of your mouth."

Micah squinched his face tight so Teddy couldn't get the glue past his lips.

"Don't want to open, huh?" Teddy got Micah in a headlock, and since he was so slight, Teddy could pinch Micah's nostrils shut with the same hand. "Well, you gotta breathe sometime, and when you do . . ." Teddy stood ready with the glue. Micah held his breath.

"Need some air yet, street rat?" Teddy taunted. Micah held his breath for longer than Teddy expected, but Teddy just laughed. "You'll need air soon, street rat."

Suddenly, just as Micah was about to turn blue from a lack of oxygen, he bit Teddy on the hand, breaking the flesh with his teeth.

"*Ow!* You little freakin' punk!"

Micah broke free and ran across the room. "Dick! Dick! Dick!"

"Oh," Teddy said with a burn in his eye. "You're dead now."

Though Micah tried to squirm away, Teddy caught

him immediately and marched him over to the other side of the room in an even tighter headlock, applying heavy pressure to the sides of Micah's ears. "Let's see how you like it when I put your nose in the pencil sharpener."

"You can't fit m' nose in dere."

"Oh, yeah? . . ."

Teddy slammed his fist down on the pencil sharpener, and the plastic casing fell off. Suddenly the pencil sharpener looked like a medieval torture machine ready to grind Micah's face off.

"You're just full of lip, ain't you, street rat? Well, let's just see how you like . . ." Teddy moved Micah's head toward the sharpener, the kid's eyes growing wider with fear. Then suddenly Micah's gaze turned toward the corner of the room. Teddy's eyes followed. Diaz had walked in. Teddy let go.

"Yeah," Micah taunted as he shook free, his ears throbbing in pain. "Good decision, nigga. 'Cause if I didn't getya, my peeps would've."

Micah threw up some gang signs, wannabe style.

Teddy shook his head.

"I think that's enough for today. Micah, why don't you take off a bit early?"

Micah grabbed his notebook, flipped Teddy the middle finger, and left. There was a pause.

"Creative mentoring I assume?"

"That kid's a lost cause."

"A lost cause . . . *Hmm*, let me think about that. Yeah, I guess you're right. That's one way to describe a child whose mother was addicted to heroin when she gave birth to him."

Teddy didn't respond.

"Actually, that's an excellent description, now that I think about it. Two older brothers in the cemetery, an older sister doing fifteen to twenty for narcotics trafficking. Forget his biological father—we're not even sure if his mom knows who he is. Plus, seven foster homes in nine years as a ward of the state. *Hmm,* I think you're right, Teddy. Good diagnosis. Micah is officially a lost cause, at the age of twelve."

Teddy looked away.

"Did you even take half a look at the file I gave you on him? Hello? This is why he's categorized as 'at-risk.' No family. Terrible role models. He's already halfway in with a gang. Plus, his grades in school have been poor for years. People call it 'attention-deficit disorder,' but that's just a label. No one's ever taken the time to figure out what the heck is really wrong. However, one thing I can tell you is he has no sense of self-worth, no self-respect. And when you don't respect yourself, you don't respect anybody else, either."

Teddy still didn't say anything.

"Basically, Micah shows every sign of being the next generation of violent gangbanger. He's even got a hardcore old-G second cousin who's a mainhead shot-caller for one of the most vicious sets in the neighborhood. Wake up, Teddy. This kid's on the edge, going to a place he'll never come back from."

"So why me? What am I supposed to do about it, huh?"

"Oh, come on, Teddy, you're smarter than that. It's so one day someone else's little sister doesn't get shot in a drive-by."

Then was silence.

Diaz walked over to the broken pencil sharpener and lifted the cracked casing. She shrugged. "Like I have the budget for that."

A moment later Diaz walked back into her office. "Have a nice afternoon, Teddy. You're free to go home early, too."

The first thing Teddy did when he arrived home was read the file on Micah. It was a primer for hell. Horrible grades. Low test scores. No family. A ward of the state. Arrested eight times. Once, Micah had even been released by the cops, with no charges filed against him, but had had to spend two nights in prison anyway because no one bothered to pick him up. No wonder Micah was about to become a gangsta. Nowhere else wanted him.

Teddy showed up the next day at Hawkins Middle School with a different look on his face.

"Back for more, Dick?"

Teddy looked at the glue on the desk but stayed calm.

"Peeps call me T-Bear. You could call me that if you want."

Micah looked up without saying anything.

"Got math homework?"

"Nope."

"Come on, dude. Every math teacher gives homework."

"School's for fools. I'm gonna be a balla'."

"A baller, huh?"

"Dat's right, a major balla' with major re-spect and juice on da' street."

"All right, Mr. Baller, well, even a drug dealer needs to know how to do math so he can count all his cash." Teddy quickly scribbled some arithmetic on a pad of paper he had brought. "Do this problem. It's long division." Micah stared at the work defiantly. "I said, do this problem." Micah still didn't make a move. "What, you don't know how? See, you take the numerator and divide by the denominator and—"

"Whassa point? My teacher just gonna fail me anyway. Punk already wrote me four referrals."

"Why? You screwin' around?"

"Naw, 'cause I ain't had a protractor."

"What do you mean, you ain't had a protractor?"

"Dat's what I'm sayin'. I ain't had a one of those plastic protractors, so he wrote me a referral to git me outta class."

"Look, dude, it's a math class. Bring your supplies, huh? You need a pencil? Here." Teddy reached into his bag and gave Micah a pencil. "Keep it. Now do this problem." Micah glowered, refusing to budge. Teddy, it appeared, had somehow just deeply insulted him. "All right, fine," Teddy said. "Don't do your math."

"Look, I don't need no favas from you. Just cuz your sis got blasted RP, RT–style don't mean you gotta do shit fo' me."

"What'd you say?" Teddy asked.

"Yeah, I know all 'bout it. I don't need no charity from you. I gots homeboyz that got my back." Micah stood and backed away from the table.

"Yeah, I know lots, fool. Like how th' only reason you here is 'cause the courts *made* you come, and soon as your time up, you gonna bail out on me jus' like everyone else. That's why I got homeboyz. They'll always be true."

For the first time, Micah didn't wait for the three o'clock bell to ring. He simply threw up a few gang signs, then headed out.

Teddy didn't stop him, either. Instead, he stormed into Diaz's office. "You told him about my sister?"

Diaz paused. "Yes, I did," she finally answered, not ashamed of having told the truth.

"That ain't right, Diaz. That ain't right at all."

"I thought it would give you some credibility with him."

"I want a new kid."

"There is no new kid."

"I want a new kid."

"Did you hear me? There is no new kid. You've got Micah, and he's got you, and that's all there is to it, unless you want to go back and face Judge Lynch."

"You're a fucking bitch," Teddy said.

Diaz raised her gaze from the work on her desk and slowly looked Teddy in the eye. Then a small grin came to her face. "Trust me, I've been called worse."

"Well, how the hell am I supposed to help a little wannabe gangbanger who doesn't even want to be helped in the first place?"

"They all want to be helped, Teddy. Even the hardcores. Listen, Teddy. My funds are drying up faster than I anticipated." There were nearly one hundred and seventy-five kids to check in with per week, every week, and the strain G-PIP was putting on the process by making so much of her time solely about just two kids for six hours a week, every week of the month, was making things very, very difficult.

Help, as Diaz knew, was clearly not on the way.

"You're still here?" Diaz said to Teddy, looking up from her pile of papers that had been causing her multiple headaches lately. "Our conversation's over."

"This is bullshit."

"Be here tomorrow."

"Kiss my ass."

"I don't have time for this, Teddy. Be here tomorrow at one thirty."

He glared at her. "Did you tell Micah how *he* died?" Teddy said, pointing to the picture of the Latino boy on Diaz's desk under which was written, IN LOVING MEMORY. . . .

Rage flashed across Diaz's eyes. "Don't you push me."

"Was it RP, RT, Diaz?"

"Shut up, Teddy."

"Did you hear the gunshots, Diaz?"

"Shut up, Teddy."

"Did you see the blood? Did you scream for help that never came?"

"I said, shut up!"

"And did you cry, Diaz? Did you cry night after night after night?"

Diaz tore open a desk drawer and and ripped out the yellow sheet of paper on which was written Teddy's name, DIXON THEODORE ANDERSON. "I'll do it, Teddy. I'll do it right now."

"But the tears never washed away the nightmares, did they, Diaz? They never washed away the terror of watching a *black* teenager gun down your brother."

"I said, *shut up!*"

"And though you don't want to admit it, the truth is, deep down, you hate black people."

"That isn't true!" she snapped.

"And all your fancy degrees, all your commendations of merit, all your badges and handcuffs and power, they still can't change one thing, can they, Diaz? They still can't change the fact that deep down you hate niggers because one of 'em took your brother away."

"You're so out of line."

"Go 'head, sign the form. I know that's what this is all about. Sign it!" Teddy shouted. "End it now. You know this is all about race. The whole criminal justice system is all about race."

Diaz brought pen to paper, the tip of the point hovering just over the line that read:

SIGNATURE: _____ .

"You know, you are right about one thing, Teddy," Diaz answered. "It did hurt. It hurt bad." She set down her pen. "And it still does. But if you think this is about race, you're wrong. When gangs kill people, the blood spills red. Latinos, African Americans, Asians, Pacific Islanders, whites, and everybody else. The blood always spills the same color, Teddy: red." Diaz recapped her pen. "Be here tomorrow," she added. "And be on time."

14

Thunderstorms smashed across the sky. Diaz looked at the clock. The time ticked from 1:29 to 1:30. No Teddy.

The rain crashed outside: 1:35 came and went. Still no Teddy.

Then 1:38. Still no Teddy. Diaz waited.

"He just a punk anyway, Officer Dee. I don't even know why you be hookin' us up like dis," Micah said, looking up from his colored-paper notebook.

Then 1:39. Diaz started slowly for the telephone, ready to make "the call." Then the door opened. In walked Teddy, soaked from the rain. Diaz waited for an excuse.

"Traffic."

She stared.

"What? You never heard of traffic? It's pissing rain out there."

Diaz hung up the phone, crossed the room, and whispered in Teddy's ear. "You've used your slack. Don't push me again." Then, with her head held high, Diaz left the room, leaving Micah and Teddy alone.

Teddy took off his raincoat and tossed it on a chair. "Wanna do math?"

"Up yours, Dick."

"That's what I thought."

Teddy flopped down in a chair, reached into his backpack, and took out an oversize Burger King bag. Inside was a Double Whopper, a large fries, a large onion rings, and a chocolate milk shake. The smell of warm food filled the room. Micah stared at a French fry.

"Don't even think about it," Teddy said.

Micah glared at Teddy, then looked down at his notebook and tried to concentrate on his drawing, but the thought of the food distracted him from his sheet of blue paper.

Teddy took a giant bite out of his Double Whopper. Ketchup dribbled down his chin. Micah couldn't help but look over. "Not even a seed from my sesame-seed bun, punk," Teddy taunted, and to make the point entirely clear, he took another huge chomp of his burger.

"You're a dick," Micah replied.

Teddy smiled and slurped his milk shake. "A-a-ah!" he added with an exaggerated expression of satisfaction to rub it in.

A moment later Diaz entered, attracted by the smell as well. She took a moment to observe the situation, then approached Micah.

"Storm's gonna get worse tonight, Micah. Why don't you go ahead and get back early. Try to stay dry if you can."

Micah stood up, tucked his pad of colored paper under his shirt, and hesitated at the door, looking out into the storm. Pellets of wetness crashed to the pavement outside. Micah turned, flipped Teddy the middle finger, and pulled the hood of his sweatshirt over his head and dashed off into the rain.

Teddy smiled and popped an onion ring into his mouth. Diaz glared. "That mean I'm off early, too?"

Diaz took a moment before answering. "Yeah, you too."

"Sweet!" Teddy said, quickly gobbling down the rest of his burger. Three gulps later the Whopper had disappeared, and Teddy started putting on his raincoat.

"You know, he's probably hungry," Diaz said.

"Well, so am I," Teddy replied, shoveling a fistful of French fries and onion rings into his mouth. Diaz shook her head. "What? What are you shaking your head for? How come women are always shaking their heads?"

"The file said you were extraordinarily perceptive."

"So?"

"So didn't you notice Micah's 'raincoat'? That's the same sweatshirt he's worn for the past three days."

Teddy paused to think about it. Throwing the hood

over the top of his head to use as a raincoat in a storm like this meant Micah didn't own a raincoat. And why was that? Probably because no one had ever bought him one. Wards of the state didn't usually end up with much of a clothing budget.

And when Diaz said Micah was probably hungry, she likely didn't mean Micah was hungry just then. She meant Micah was hungry the way a kid is hungry when he usuallly doesn't eat three meals a day. The boy was skinny as a pipe cleaner, and foster homes in the 'hood were notorious for taking the funds they received for each child's food budget and making the money disappear into flat screen televisions and long weekends in Vegas.

"See you tomorrow, Teddy," Diaz said, walking back into her office.

Teddy didn't answer. He grabbed his stuff and left.

At one thirty the next day, the rain was still pouring down from the skies. Teddy entered the room and tossed down his raincoat.

"You wanna do math?"

"Up yours, Dick."

"That's what I thought."

Teddy reached into his backpack, took out a Burger King bag, and set it on the table. The smell of hot French fries filled the air. Micah tried not to stare at the food. Teddy grabbed a chocolate shake and crossed the room.

A moment later, Micah lowered his eyes and started to doodle.

"Well, go 'head. There's fries and a burger in there for you, too."

Micah paused. Then he leaped for the bag. "Ain't gotta tell me twice."

"Mine's the one with no pickles. Yours is no onions. It's written on the wrapper."

Micah shoveled a handful of fries into his mouth. Teddy couldn't help but smile when he saw how greedily the kid began gobbling them down.

"Why yours ain't got no pickles?" Micah asked, unloading the bag.

"'Cause I hate pickles," Teddy answered. "And you get no onions 'cause I don't want your breath to stink."

"Whatta 'bout yo' breath?" he asked.

"Hey," Teddy replied. "I ain't the one who's gotta smell it."

Micah grimaced. Teddy laughed. "I couldn't carry two chocolate shakes, so we'll just split this one if I can find a cup to— Hey, I said no pickles was for me."

The wrappers on both burgers were clearly

labeled in black grease pencil. Micah stopped just before he took a bite out of the wrong burger and tried to cover his tracks. "Sorry, oh yeah, I forgot." He set the burger down with a look of shame in his eyes and quietly picked up the other Whopper, taking only a small bite. A moment later Teddy brought over the extra cup he'd found in the cabinet.

"All good, dude?" Teddy asked, pouring half the shake into the cup.

There was a pause. "Yep," Micah responded. "All good, T.B."

"What?" Teddy asked.

"Yeah, T.B. You know, fo' T-Bear," Micah answered.

Teddy thought about it for a moment. No one had ever called him "T.B." before, but after repeating it to himself once in his head, Teddy had to admit he didn't mind the sound of it too much. And it was certainly better than being called "Dick" for the next sixteen thousand hours he owed the state. The two ate for a moment in silence.

"We doin' math next," Teddy said.

"Aw, come on, T.B.—screw math."

Teddy looked at Micah chowing down on the burger as if it were the tastiest thing he had ever put into his mouth.

"Naw, li'l homie, we doin' math."

When Teddy arrived home, he, as usual, jumped directly onto the computer. But instead of logging into Mrs. Wellman's zombie machine to double-check his district accounting scam, Teddy logged into the CLETS database to research Micah's academic history.

Throughout his years in school, Micah had accumulated a sea of F's in all his classes. Teddy began to dig a little deeper and soon discovered that Micah's third-grade teacher had suspected he had a learning disability and requested he get tested. He never was.

Teddy could find no reason for why Micah had never been tested, but the answer was probably simple: budget cuts. Teddy thought, how many times have I heard that before?

The lack of money, Teddy knew, kept thousands and thousands of inner-city kids like Micah from getting the educational services they needed. Inner-city residents complained all the time that the federal government seemed to have money for bombs, money for wars, money for jails, and money to compensate

159

for tax breaks for the rich, but there was never enough money for poor urban schools.

Teddy sat back and paused. It was the first time he had ever looked at one of the system's losers so up close and personal before.

Once again a clear pattern appeared to Teddy. Micah's chaotic home life and lack of education would eventually translate to unemployment. No job would mean no money. No money would mean no survival. But Teddy knew that human beings are made to survive, and if you push them far enough, they will do whatever they have to do in order to make it in this world.

As Diaz had said, it was easy to see where Micah was headed: gangland. Micah seemed doomed to join the swarms of homeboyz plaguing the streets. Someday soon he would step up to replace an older homeboy who had either been locked away in jail or gone out KIA—Killed in Action. Once you were in a gang, you were headed for either the penitentiary or the morgue. And even in the big house, gangs were everywhere.

Teddy's thoughts were interrupted by the sound of Pops coming through the front door. His father looked tired. It was nearly nine o'clock and he was just getting home from a day that had started before seven in the morning. There was no *How was your day?* There was no *Can't you do something else besides bang on that computer?* There was no *Did you take the trash out?* Nothing.

Pops put Teddy's dinner down on the counter, a fast-food chicken combo, and headed for his bedroom to change out of his clothes. It was the second night in a row that Pops had brought home the exact same meal for Teddy.

Pops wasn't stupid. He knew what he had done. Yet, the chicken-combo plate was the easiest meal he could figure out to get for his son on his way home, where he would take a shower and collapse into bed next to his wife, a woman who had become a ghost of her former self.

Though they didn't speak a word, Teddy knew that many things were weighing on Pops's mind, none more so than the distress of the woman he had married almost thirty years ago. Mrs. Anderson insisted on attending every day of Maggot's trial, and it was taking an excruciating toll on her. Regardless of the emotional pain watching the trial inflicted, she sat through every motion, every proceeding, and every last bit of legalese that the lawyers wrestled through. None of the Andersons could understand why she felt the need to put herself through this torture.

Maggot's attorney claimed that his client was a

victim of police conspiracy, that his client had an alibi, that his client's rights were being violated, that his client had been merely an easy target of a police quest to catch a gangsta—any gangsta—in order to make the citizens feel safe and to satisfy the bloodthirsty media. The lawyer even claimed that it was really the ineptitude of the police department and the criminal justice system that should be on trial. All this was almost unbearable for Mrs. Anderson to listen to, but still she sat through it all.

At first Pops had tried to talk her out of it. But Tina's murder had cracked Mrs. Anderson in a way that alarmed Pops deeply. She was beyond grief. Everyone around her felt that she had been fractured. Though she had always loved to cook, she hadn't prepared a meal in months. She had become sloppy in her dress, too, leaving home in outfits that didn't match, and wearing fuzzy slippers out instead of real shoes—things she never would have done before Tina's death.

Then one day Pops came home from work early to grab a phone number he had forgotten on his desk and saw his wife, standing in her slip in the bedroom, staring at the bed. Just staring at it with a perplexed look on her face.

"Honey," Pops asked nervously. "What's . . . what's going on?"

"I forgot how to make the bed," Mrs. Anderson replied, staring straight ahead emptily. "I forgot how to make the bed," she repeated.

Pops discovered that she had been standing there for more than three hours, tucking in the sheets, folding down the blankets, fluffing the pillows, smoothing out the edges of the pillowcases—over and over again. But none of it made any sense to her. All Mrs. Anderson could say after her hours of effort was "I forgot how to make the bed."

Pops persuaded her to take an unpaid leave of absence from her job at the bank, and she began to see a therapist. The therapist, however, had wanted to put her on medication, but she refused, quit seeing the therapist, and instead continued with her own self-prescribed therapy: attending the trial of the boy accused of murdering her daughter. And when Mrs. Anderson wasn't in court, she slept.

Financial problems prevented Pops from being able to join his wife in court to sit beside her every day. The Anderson family couldn't afford to miss both parents' paychecks, and the extra work added to Pops's stress. Now he had to make ends meet alone, while running the household, too.

Take-out had become a way of life for the Andersons—fried chicken, Chinese food, burgers, and pizza. It was a terrible diet for Pops, who had suffered from both high cholesterol and high blood pressure for several years. Yet, what else was he to do? Pops certainly wasn't a cook, and with all the running around he already had to do as Teddy's court-appointed chauffeur, it was all Pops could do to keep his business going.

Pops owned a linen delivery company whose main clients were twenty-seven local Italian restaurants—lots of red-sauce stains. Pops had originally started out with a simple pickup laundry service, cleaning the restaurants' tablecloths and napkins for them, but after a year and a half, he had figured out that it was even more profitable to buy the linens himself and rent them out to the restaurants with laundering included. Over the course of seventeen years, Pops had built his business up, and now had three vans and six employees. He had earned a reputation for dependability, quality, and consistency. He was a respected local businessman.

Since Tina's death, however, his customers had grown frustrated with Pops's erratic work. Normally prompt and efficient, Pops was getting orders wrong and mixing up his scheduled pickup and drop-off times. His concern for his wife and son was making him absentminded, distant, and grouchy. It was hardly surprising that he had resorted to dropping bags of fast food on the kitchen counter, knowing Teddy would wolf down his meals on his own time.

Teddy said nothing about being served the exact same meal for the second night in a row. His father had already had one heart attack, and judging by the way Pops had just dragged himself through the front door, Teddy thought it was only a matter of time before he had another.

Pops had recently lost his biggest client, a small chain of five Italian restaurants he had been servicing for thirteen and a half years. "I'm sorry about your problems, but I have a business to run," the owner had explained. And to make matters worse, he had transferred his account to Pops's biggest competitor. Money pressures were about to increase.

Teddy heard the door to his parents' bedroom close. He looked at the sagging bag holding his dinner on the counter, turned, and went back to his computer. His parents' world was crumbling, but he had work to do.

16

Teddy arrived early the next day to chat privately with Diaz. "I don't think Micah can read," he said.

Diaz didn't even raise her eyes from her paperwork. "Probably not," she answered. This information wasn't nearly the shock for her Teddy thought it would be.

"But how can a kid get to eighth grade if he can't read?"

"It's called social promotion. The schools can't have seventh-grade boys who are going through puberty sitting in classes with fourth-grade girls, so even if the kids don't have the academic skills, they get pushed up through the system to the next grade level."

"They just move 'em through?"

"Pretty much. It's like a factory out there."

Teddy stood silent, unsure of how to respond.

"You're surprised by this?" Diaz asked.

"No. I mean, I guess I saw it, but I just never really *saw* it, you know."

"And all those tests they make the kids take, in fourth grade for instance, they aren't just tests to see what their aptitudes are. The state uses some of those results to forecast how many prisons they'll need to build over the next decade."

"You mean they use school test scores to determine how many jail cells they will need to build for the next generation of convicts?"

"Exactly. You're a stats whiz; take a look at it sometime. Look at the number of fourth-grade minority boys reading way below grade level, factor in the level of community poverty at which they live, and the percentage of their parents who have been or are currently in prison. Add it all up and you'll have a pretty good indicator of how many jail cells the state is going to need to accommodate all of these kids, since they will likely grow up to be felons."

"Well, why the hell don't they just put the money into education and prevent the crimes from happening in the first place?"

"Ask the people who make the decisions. Our schools are overcrowded and underfunded. Some of them lack even the most basic resources. Teaching is notoriously one of the most underpaid professions, which means we don't attract the best and brightest minds to the classroom. What kind of crazy person do you have to be to take a job as an inner-city teacher today?" Diaz couldn't help but laugh and shake her head. "And people wonder why we're in the mess we're in. How do they expect it to work out?" She paused. "What's wrong, Teddy?"

"It's fucking depressing, that's what's wrong," he answered.

"Aw, you gotta learn to look at the bright side."

"What bright side?"

"I don't know," Diaz answered. "Each person has to find it for himself."

A moment later, Micah walked in. Or rather, he floated. "What's up, T.B.? Hey-hey, Officer Dee." Micah was bursting with energy. He slapped Teddy a high-five, picked Diaz's police badge off her desk, shined it on his shirt, then returned the badge to the desk freshly polished, his eyes beaming.

"Why you all charged up today?" Teddy asked.

"I got a B on my science quiz," he answered. "Look!" Micah proudly held up his score.

"No way, let me see." Micah handed a green sheet of paper to Teddy. "Sweet, dude."

But Teddy was perplexed. Hadn't they been talking only a moment ago about how Micah seemed to be unable to read? Yet here he was passing a science quiz that was asking him to respond to questions about a short reading comprehension passage concerning how electric current travels across a wire. Teddy stared at Micah's quiz, flipping the dilemma over in his mind. *Maybe it's a subject-matter thing?* he said to himself. *No, that doesn't make sense.*

"What we got today, Burger King or McDonald's? I'm hungry like a pit bull," Micah said. Without bothering to ask permission, Micah opened up Teddy's backpack, grabbed a burger, and tossed a few fries in his mouth.

"This ain't got pickles, right? I mean, you knows I hate pickles, T.B." Diaz and Teddy just stared at Micah in silence. "What? What ya'll lookin' at?"

"Just eat, dude," Teddy answered. "Just eat."

The following day, Teddy showed up for their regular meeting with more than just Burger King.

"Read this."

"Come on, I hate reading."

"Just read it to me."

Micah stared at the words but didn't speak. He clearly didn't want to embarrass himself.

"What if I do this?" Teddy asked as he slid a transparent yellow plastic sheet across the page. Suddenly, Micah's eyes got wide and he started reading easily.

" 'Halloween is one of our most famous holidays in the United States. People carve pumpkins and make funny faces on them. These are called jack-o'-lanterns. On October thirty-first of every year, children put on special costumes, dressing up as a witch, ghost, or clown, for example, and knock on the doors of houses saying . . ."

All of a sudden, Micah was reading without any problem. Diaz entered. "What's going on?" she asked.

"This," Teddy said, reaching for the science quiz Micah had scored a B on, which they had hung on the wall in a gesture of pride. "The teacher was probably out of white paper."

"So?" asked Diaz.

"Think about it, the colored-paper construction book he loves to draw in, the B on this quiz, the hamburger wrapper. Micah, dude, I've got good news and bad."

"What's the bad news?"

"You suffer from dyslexia."

"I do?"

"But the good news is, I think we can beat it." Teddy reached into his backpack and pulled out a sheet of paper he had printed off of the Internet. "Check it out."

WHAT DYSLEXIA LOOKS LIKE

The text on the right was read through a colored overlay.

"I see lots of letters reversed."	*"The letters are facing the right way."*
ꙅbɿɒwʞɔɒd llɒ	all backwards
"I see the words all wrong."	*"The words look right."*
too many	too many
"The letters change around."	*"Now they stay the right way."*
hrad to raed	hard to read
"Sometimes I don't see some of the letters."	*"This looks good! I can see the letters. It's got more space."*
misng ltrs	missing letters

"Hey, that's what it looks like to me," Micah said, pointing at an example on the sheet. "You mean it don't look dat way to all y'all?"

"Uh . . . no," said Diaz.

"It's not the words themselves that cause Micah trouble, it's the black-on-white text. Color overlays make things more clear for him. Many dyslexic people have difficulty processing black-on-white text."

Diaz held up the yellow overlay. "Our supply budget—"

"These things cost about thirty-eight cents," Teddy interjected, throwing a package of plastic overlays in the colors of the rainbow down on the desk. "Here's a pack of ten, dude, to get you started."

Diaz sat in a chair and shook her head. "You mean to tell me that a simple thirty-eight-cent color overlay might be the key to keeping a kid like Micah out of jail?"

"I ain't goin' a jail. I ain't did nothin'!"

"No, I know you're not, Micah. It's just a point I was making to Teddy. How many other kids do you think suffer from this problem?"

"Some say it affects up to ten percent of the population. It troubles all kinds of people regardless of intelligence, race, or class. Lots of times there are effective ways to work around it, but first dyslexia's

172

gotta be diagnosed. Many people who struggle with reading have been told they are stupid for so long that they simply believe it, and never get help." Teddy turned to Micah. "Ain't that right, Li'l Stoop?"

Micah lowered his eyes. "That just what otha' folks call me. I ain't never called myself dat."

"Well, you need a new street name."

"Like what?"

"I don't know," Teddy answered. "We'll figure something out."

Micah crossed to the counter where the extra cups were kept.

"All right, I'm down with dat, but since we talkin' 'bout changin' things, we gotta start changin' the fact that you ain't bringin' me my own chocolate shake. This sharin' a shake nonsense be gettin' old."

Micah started to pour half the milk shake into a cup. And while he could have made the servings uneven, he never did. Every time he split the milk shakes into two cups, he always poured exactly even amounts for himself and Teddy.

"Just hurry up and eat, dude. You got social studies homework to do."

Diaz continued to stare at the color overlay. "You did well, Teddy."

"Good enough to start driving again?"

"Don't push it."

"Aw, come on, Diaz, this schedule is just killin' my pops."

Diaz paused to think about it. "Okay, but you're still on house probation. Work, then here, then back home. No exceptions."

"Cool," Teddy replied. Diaz and Teddy made eye contact. After looking up, Teddy looked away, not going so far as to say thanks.

That afternoon, the entire world changed for Micah. Not only could he read, but without all the jumbled, illegible letters to deal with, Micah discovered he kind of liked reading because it made him feel smarter. Teddy watched Micah's self-esteem balloon.

Over the next two weeks a pattern emerged. Micah and Teddy would each eat a Double Whopper—no onions or pickles—and Micah would then work to get caught up in all of his classes, especially science. Micah really liked his science teacher and wanted to do a particularly strong job on an upcoming report.

"So what do you want to do it on?"

"Bugs."

"Bugs?" asked Teddy.

"Yeah, bugs."

As it turned out, Micah loved bugs. Especially the nasty, gnarly ones.

"Look how cool this one is," Micah said, pointing to a revolting picture of a Scarabaeinae beetle in an encyclopedia Teddy had brought from home.

"You sure you want to do that one? I mean, that's a dung beetle, dude. You know what that means they eat, don't you?"

Micah flipped the page in the book, laid a green overlay down over the words, and searched for the answer. Teddy didn't ask the question as a real question, he meant it rhetorically, but Micah took it as a research challenge, and once Micah set his mind to doing something, Teddy had learned that he was going to stick with it until he found what he was looking for.

Teddy waited while Micah turned another page in the book. Each time Micah flipped the page he had to remove the green overlay, then lay it down afresh over the new words he wanted to read. But Micah didn't care about the extra effort. He could finally read.

"The book says they . . ." Micah had to sound out the words. " 'They eat new . . . nutrient-rich ex-cre-ment.' Nutrient-rich excrement. What's that?" Micah asked.

"It means they eat shit," Teddy answered.

"They do?" replied Micah. *"Cooool!"*

"You're disgusting, dude."

"Man, I gotta know this stuff."

"Right," Teddy answered. "You're a regular ol' entomologist."

Micah wrinkled his brow in confusion. "What's dat?"

"It's a bug scientist," Teddy replied.

"Yeah, that sounds like somethin' cool," Micah responded as a smile spread across his face. "Maybe one day I'll be an ento-ma-whatever-ya-call-it."

"An entomologist."

"Yeah, an en-to-mol-o-gist," Micah repeated, still smiling. Then he turned to the next page and laid his green overlay on a different passage about Scarabaeinae beetles.

A moment later, Micah paused and looked up. "Yo, T.B., can I ask ya a question?"

"Yeah, wassup?"

Micah paused, then looked over his shoulder to make sure Diaz wasn't in the room. "Is oral sex, sex?"

"What?"

"I mean, if I can get a girl to, ya know . . . give my lollipop some lovin', am I still a virgin?"

"Why are you asking?"

"'Cause I don't want to be no virgin," Micah said, looking hurt. "Niggas be makin' fun of me back at the fosta' home."

Teddy closed the book in front of him and looked Micah straight in the eye.

"Micah, let me tell you somethin', li'l homie. You don't want to be using the word *niggas* the way you do."

"Why not, it's what everyone be sayin'. All it means is some shit like 'brothas' or 'homies' or somethin' like that."

"No, it means *niggers*—no matter how you say it, no matter how you spell it. And before you interrupt, I don't care what kind of bullshit you hear from other folks about how it doesn't mean what it used to mean. They're wrong. *Niggas* means 'niggers,' and it's a word that represents slavery. Did you know that back in the day when black people were being lynched, the word *niggers* was often the last word they heard before they swung from the end of a rope?" Micah looked down in shame. "You say you want to be an entomologist? Go try to get a job using the word *nigga* in the interview. Hell, they won't even hire you to sweep the floor."

"Damn, T.B., why you goin' all deep on me?"

Teddy paused. Yeah, why was he going all deep on Micah? The answer popped into Teddy's mind, but he didn't want to acknowledge it. "Just don't use it. Jews don't call themselves 'kikes.' Asians don't call themselves 'gooks.' Latinos don't call themselves 'spics.' Only black people call themselves 'niggas.' So even if everyone else is doin' it, don't. We gotta find a way to make things better for us. It's hard on peeps like us, ya know?" Teddy paused, looking Micah straight in the eye. "I said," Teddy repeated, "ya know?"

"Yeah," Micah replied. "I know."

17

Over the next few days, Micah started bringing in ladybugs, caterpillars, and any sort of insect he could find. And Diaz was *not* a fan of his bug project in any way whatsoever.

"Just look at it, Officer Dee. It's only a cock-a-roach," Micah said as he let the creature walk over his fingers.

"Micah, I am warning you, get that out of my office . . . *now!*"

Micah's science project had been assigned as an oral presentation, and while everything was taking great shape, he still felt he could do more research to make his project more, as he said, "Dyn-na-ma-tastic!"

However, in order to get Micah what he really needed, Teddy knew they'd have to go to the library. But for that they'd need permission from Diaz.

"Use the school library," Diaz said, when Teddy asked her about it.

"The school library sucks," Micah answered. "They ain't got no books, and there be graffiti in all the encyclopedias."

"It's true," Teddy confirmed.

Pops had often quoted an old saying in the restaurant business: If you want to know how good a restaurant's food is, all you have to do is taste their bread, because a great restaurant never serves terrible bread, and a terrible restaurant never serves great bread. The same could be said of school libraries, Teddy thought. If you want to know how good a school is, just look at the library. A great school never has a terrible library, and a terrible school never has a great library. And inner-city middle schools were notorious for having underfunded, understaffed, underresourced libraries full of big-hearted librarians doing their best to win an unwinnable war.

"The public library I was thinking of taking him to is pretty awesome and will have tons of reference materials I'm sure he'd love to see."

Diaz thought about it. "Do you have a library card?" she asked.

"Who, me?" Teddy answered. "I have six library cards . . . in three different names with five different addresses." Diaz glared at him. "Just kidding, Diaz. Yes, I have a library card."

"How are you going to get there?" Diaz asked, with a suspicious edge in her voice.

"I'll drive him." Teddy answered.

"But it's almost three o'clock, the bell is going to ring any minute."

Teddy and Micah looked at each other. "I got no place to be," Teddy said.

"Me either," Micah added.

There was a long pause.

"But . . ." Teddy added, pulling up the left leg of his jeans to show Diaz the ankle bracelet.

"Yo, you got one of them, too, T.B.?" Micah exclaimed with a huge smile as he pulled up the left leg of his own jeans as well. "Ha-ha, we like the gangsta twins and shit!"

Teddy knew from the CLETS records that Micah was under electronically enhanced supervision like himself, but Diaz had slapped the ankle bracelet on Micah for truancy more than anything else. At one point the year before, Micah had missed thirty-seven days of class in a row. During that time he'd been pinched for a few minor crimes such as shoplifting, vandalism, and the like. However, Diaz knew that was how all li'l homeboyz started. Shoplifting eventually led to robbery, which eventually turned to carjacking, then breaking and entering, then gunfire and murder. Kids in the 'hood didn't just magically turn into criminals overnight, they slid down a long, slippery slope. Micah's ankle bracelet was more than just a monitoring device, it was a small tool intended to function as a big deterrent.

The more Diaz thought about this proposed trip to the library, the more she found no reason why the two of them shouldn't go. Their request made sense. And if Micah did well on his report, it would boost his grades and provide some of the positive data for the G-PIP program that Diaz desperately needed to justify the funding. "All right, the twins get a day pass," she said at last.

"Cool!" Micah exclaimed, crossing the room to gather his belongings. With Micah's attention diverted elsewhere, Diaz pulled Teddy to the side and spoke in a whisper. "If it's getting dark by the time you're done, make sure you drive him back to his foster home and watch him until he walks through the front door. It's not safe for him at night, even if it is only five thirty. Homeboyz are everywhere around where he stays."

"All right," Teddy answered.

"Micah, here, take this," Diaz said, handing him a cell phone and charger.

"Sweet, Officer Dee!" Micah replied. "Yo, T.B., I got me a cell phone." Micah flipped open the phone and pretended to dial. "I'm-a call Thailand and order me a pizza."

"It's a coded phone for emergencies, Micah, and

nothing else," Diaz explained. "If you ever need me, just press the number sign, then two-four, and I'll get an immediate pager alert."

"And the good guys'll come and save me and shit, right?" Micah answered with a smile.

"Yeah, something like that," Diaz answered.

Micah put the cell phone in his pocket and headed for the door.

"Come on, T.B., hustle up. Let's *roll,* dogg," Micah said.

Teddy made a move to follow. Diaz grabbed him by the arm. "Hey, Teddy . . ." she said with a serious look on her face. "I am only going to tell you this one time. Don't screw this up."

Though Teddy couldn't believe it when he heard it, this was going to be Micah's first time ever inside a public library.

"Dang, look at all da' stuff," Micah commented. "They got music, magazines, videos, computers, comic books, and the Internet, too?"

"Dude, they got it all. We'll even hook you up with a library card before we go."

"I could get one? Like I don't need me a credit card or none of that?"

"Nope, it's free."

"Sweet!" replied Micah. Fifteen minutes later Teddy and Micah were sitting at a dark wooden table under a green lamp in soft, padded chairs. Not a scratch of graffiti, tagging, or a crew's name was carved in the wood anywhere on the table where ten reference books lay spread out in front of them.

Micah shifted his color overlays all over the place, going from book to book to book, soaking up information like a sponge. Unfortunately, Micah didn't really have a system of organization, and he often recopied pieces of information he had already written down, but when Teddy tried to lend a helping hand, Micah stubbornly pushed him away. It would have been a lot faster if Micah had allowed Teddy to do the research, organize the notes, and identify the key points for his project—and Teddy would have done it, too—but Micah wanted to do it all by himself. Micah didn't care if Teddy was a supergenius; he was determined to do every bit of work on his own.

"I ain't stupid, ya know. I can do this."

"I know, Ento. I know."

"Ento?" Micah asked.

"Yeah, you know. Your new a.k.a. Short for *Entomologist*."

Micah paused. "Yeah, I'm kinda feelin' that."

Realizing that Micah wasn't going to let Teddy help

him, and knowing that he would need a good amount of time to get his project notes together, Teddy decided to slip off and use one of the library's computers with Internet access. He could access his "Type II Special Services" account from any Web-connected computer on the planet without leaving a trace. Teddy started to link a chain of proxy servers to route his login through servers in Argentina, Thailand, and Holland.

But then he stopped.

Teddy knew his scam was rolling perfectly well, without a hitch. There was no need to check it again.

Then Teddy thought about checking in for an update on Maggot, to see what evil things might await him in the prison system. Maybe a fresh idea of ways to torment Maggot would come to mind, and Teddy could start laying out a new plan. But then he didn't do that either.

Teddy also considered spying on the private e-mail of his former high-school principal, or putting out a false arrest warrant for domestic abuse for the man who had just canceled his contract with Pops's company. But he didn't.

Instead, with at least half an hour at his disposal and the entire Internet at the tips of his fingers, Teddy pushed his chair back from the terminal and crossed to the magazine section, where a *Sports Illustrated* cover story on USC football caught his eye. Though Teddy and his sister Tee-Ay had fought bitterly over many things in the past, USC football had never been one of them. Teddy had always loved the USC Trojans.

A few minutes later Teddy cruised back over to sit beside Micah, a magazine under his arm and plenty of time to read it. This beats the hell out of house arrest, he thought as he got comfortable in his chair.

"Yo, T.B., did you know that bugs are the largest group of animals on Earth?"

"Naw, didn't know that," Teddy answered, opening to the article about the ferocious Trojan defense.

"And that they got lots of important jobs, like helpin' to spread pollen and seeds so new plants can grow?"

Teddy flipped the pages, casually reading along. "Naw, didn't know that, either."

"Plus, lots of animals eat insects. If bugs disappeared, most people and animals would too."

"Nope, didn't know that," Teddy replied absent-mindedly, trying to read.

"And ya know what else? Bugs can—"

"Micah," Teddy snapped. "This bug stuff is startin' to bug me. Do your work, dude. I'm tryin' to kick it here."

Micah paused and glared at Teddy, a flash of anger raged in his eyes. Then he cracked a smile and continued right along. "And did you also know that there are more species of insects on the planet than there are varieties of flowers? And that some bugs can fly, while others can't? I ain't sure why certain types make noise, though. Like, I wonder, do ya think bugs can hear each other, as if they got ears and voices and shit?"

Teddy rolled his eyes and looked back down at the magazine. Just then, two hot girls walked past, both of them scoping out Teddy.

"Yo, T.B.," Micah said in a hushed voice, "those bitches are checkin' you out." Teddy shot Micah a glare. "Sorry—I mean, those *girls* are checkin' you out. But they were like all *bam-bam*—sizin' you up. And they were hot!"

Teddy leaned forward, not looking back at the girls. Having hot women check him out was nothing new to him.

"That reminds me," Teddy said, reaching into his backpack, "I brought you something." He slid a condom across the library table. "I never answered that sex question of yours. Look, if you're gonna do it, there are only two rules that—"

"You ever done it, T.B.?" Micah asked, interrupting Teddy before he could finish.

Teddy paused. "Yeah, I have."

"Like, how many times. Once?" Micah asked with eagerness.

"More than that," Teddy confessed.

"Twice?" Micah asked.

"More."

"Five times," Micah continued, growing more and more impressed.

"Dude, let's put it this way, if you had a tree for every time I've done it, your ass would be living in a forest."

"Da-a-amn!" Micah said, jumping out of his chair.

"*Sshhh*, sit down, dude, I'm trying to tell you something here. Two rules. First, when the time comes, use a rubber. Any fool can poke his pecker around, but it takes a man to be a father, and trust me, you ain't near ready for that yet. Hell, I ain't even near ready for that yet. Plus, there's all kinds of crazy diseases out there that can make your nuts turn purple and fall off like dead grapes, so make sure you slap one of these things on before you do any pumpin', ya got me?"

Micah held the square package up to the light, looking it over top to bottom, right and left. Just then a librarian walked past and saw Micah examining the condom.

Teddy reached over and pushed Micah's hand down. "Yo, be cool. No need to show it to the whole universe."

Micah put the rubber down on the table, then placed his color overlay on the condom's wrapper and started reading it.

"What's a . . ." Micah paused to sound out the word. "A sper-ma-side-al tip?"

"Second thing?" Teddy continued, disregarding the question. "Treat women with respect."

Micah paused, expecting more. "That's it?"

"That's it."

"I thought you was about to go all deep on me again."

"Look, one day your time is gonna come with the ladies, and while you're allowed to play the field if that's what you want to do while you're single, don't lie to women. And don't call 'em bitches and ho's, and not respect them for who they are. They deserve better. You do these things and you'll have done all right."

"I don't even think I wanna play the field, T.B.," Micah answered. "I'd rather just meet someone special, ya know, like fall in love and be with her the rest o' my life."

Teddy paused, just looking at Micah.

"What?" Micah said.

"Dude, the ladies are gonna love you," Teddy answered. "Yo, what are you doin'?" He suddenly exclaimed as Micah started tearing open the condom's wrapper. "Don't open it right here."

"Why not? I wanna put it on."

"Micah, that ain't for—"

"Naw, I'm just playin', homie," Micah responded with his mischievious laugh. "I'll wait till later then see how it fits. You'll score me more of these, right?"

Teddy looked to his left, then nodded.

"Just make sure that when it comes time that you need 'em, you use 'em."

"Yo, can we get my card now? I'm pretty solid with the info I got."

"Let's do it," Teddy answered, and ten minutes later, Micah Matthew Whitehall had his own library card to go along with his own condom, both of which had just become tied for first place as his most prized possession.

18

"I got two kinda favorite insects. Wanna know what they is?"

"Do I have a choice?" Teddy answered as he drove along, focusing on the road while scanning the streets.

Micah and Teddy were cruising through gang territory, some of the thickest in the city, and Teddy knew it was all too easy to get caught slippin' in this part of town. In the blink of an eye a thug could jump off the corner, put a Gatt to Teddy's head, and carjack him. Or a car full of homeboyz could roll up, mad dogg him, start claiming their 'hood, and begin poppin' caps without any provocation whatsoever. Even an underweight, undersize drug addict who mumbles to himself as he aimlessly walks the sidewalks might suddenly jump out and attack the car with a rusty blade. Some dope fiends would do anything if they thought it could help them score their next fix. A host of reasons explained why regular people avoided being out on these streets once day turned to night. Danger lurked in every shadow. Teddy knew this and kept a vigilant eye.

Micah, on the other hand, sat in the passenger seat entirely unconcerned. He wasn't stressed about where they were, or about what was happening around him. This was his 'hood, the streets he called home. Crazy things happened all the time.

"My first favorite be spiders," Micah continued. "They the coolest bugs ever. Guess the other."

"I don't want to guess the other."

"Guess the other."

"I said, I don't want to guess the other."

"A'right, I'll tell you," Micah said. "But promise not to laugh."

"I'm not promising nothing."

"Butterflies," Micah answered.

"Butterflies?" Teddy answered.

"Yo, you promised not to laugh."

"Naw, I just never really thought of them as bugs before."

"That's why," Micah told him. "See, they start as bugs, but then they grow into somethin' more beautiful."

Teddy turned his head and watched Micah flip through the notebook he held in his hand, not even realizing he had just said something poetic.

"It's dis house here," Micah said, pointing to the right.

Teddy pulled up to the curb and caught his first look at Micah's foster home. Dirt for a front lawn. Iron bars on all the windows and doors. A broken-down car on cinder blocks in the driveway that looked as if it had been sitting there for years. The house was one of the most ramshackle places Teddy had ever seen. He killed the lights and turned off the ignition. A lone lightbulb, dim and yellow, lit the pathway to the porch. Just walking from the car to the front door looked dangerous.

Micah unbuckled his seat belt and paused. Neither he nor Teddy seemed to know how to say good-bye. A few seconds passed.

"Yo, you hungry?" Teddy said. "We could go to my house."

"Let's do it!" Micah shot back quick as lightning as he buckled his seat belt and prepared for Teddy to take off once again. Teddy couldn't help but smile.

"Shouldn't you tell them you won't be home for dinner?" Teddy asked as he started his car. "It's getting late."

"Like they care. They'll jus' assume I got arrested or somethin'," Micah replied. "Damn, I'm hungry. I sure hope your mom can cook."

Teddy put the car in gear and pulled away from the curb. Micah's words had triggered an idea.

* * *

Teddy knew Pops would have had no idea about picking up any extra food for Micah. The smart thing would have been for Teddy to stop at a drive-through and grab something for them both to eat. But Teddy did the smarter thing and kept on driving. Ten minutes later they arrived at his driveway.

"Yo, dis where you live?" Micah asked as Teddy pulled up to the house. "This place looks sweeeeet."

Teddy took a moment and imagined seeing his home through Micah's eyes. Though it was dark outside, two well-placed yard lights lit up the front lawn. The grass was green and nicely trimmed. The wood of the front door had been restained a chocolate brown the year before, every tile on the roof was lined up as squarely as soldiers on parade, and the tall hedges running along each side of the house were trimmed tight and neat, creating the impression of a natural fence between the Andersons' home and the neighboring properties. As Micah and Teddy walked the well-lit path toward the front door, Teddy, for the first time in his life, realized why his father might not have wanted to move when the idea had come up during their family conference a few years ago. This was Pops's home, his roots. It was a place where he had toiled and sweated, loved his wife, raised his children, built a life.

From the plumbing to the painting to every picture on every wall for more than twenty years, Pops had given everything to this one address. Walking away just like that, Teddy realized, might not have been as easy as it sounded.

Teddy unlocked the front door and entered. In the living room Pops sat in his favorite chair, half watching TV, half dozing, with the volume on the television turned up extra loud to accommodate his poor hearing.

"I'm home, Pops," Teddy called out to his father, who hadn't heard the front door open. "And I brought Micah."

"Huh, who?" said Pops, waking from his daze.

"Micah. His name is *Micah!*" Teddy shouted, loud enough for the whole house to hear. He turned to Micah. "Don't mind him, dude. My father's a bit hard of hearing. Be right back. I gotta pee."

And just like that, Teddy was gone, quickly disappearing toward the bathroom and leaving Micah and Pops suddenly alone. It was an awkward moment, tense and uncertain. Especially for Micah.

Pops rose from his chair and approached his young visitor. Micah swallowed hard, trying to hide the lump in his throat.

Though a few gray hairs had sprouted in his head

and a few more wrinkles had formed around his eyes, Pops was still a solid man, strong and well built. He towered over Micah, looking him over top to bottom. An intimidating moment passed.

"You the boy Teddy works with at the middle school?"

"Yes, sir."

"How old are you?"

"Twelve."

"How are you grades?"

"Mostly F's." Pops wrinkled his forehead. "But they're starting to improve," Micah added.

Pops didn't seem very impressed. Another long moment passed before Pops resumed his questions.

"You take drugs?"

"I have."

"How many times?"

"Lots."

"When?"

"Took my first hit of weed when I was eight years old."

"Eight years old? Hot damn, boy, ain't you got no—"

"Willard!" A voice suddenly shouted from the other room. "You leave that child alone!"

Pops and Micah both turned at the same time. It

was Mrs. Anderson, dressed in a blue bathrobe and brown slippers. She started to walk slowly toward the center of the room. Mrs. Anderson hardly ever called her husband by his first name, and when she did, despite his partial deafness, Pops never failed to hear it. Mrs. Anderson retied her bathrobe belt and surveyed the situation like a four-star military general getting a first look at his troops and the battlefield ahead.

Micah was thin and raggedy, but he had nice hands—though his fingernails could have used both a cleaning and a clipping. Mrs. Anderson, like Pops, paused before she spoke. Though she had mostly locked herself inside her bedroom for the past few months, Mrs. Anderson was not unaware of what was going on in Teddy's life.

"What'd you say your name was, child?" she asked.

Micah lowered his eyes in shame, tears starting to form in his eyes. "Micah, ma'am," he responded in a low voice. When will Teddy reappear? he wondered.

Little did Micah know that Teddy was actually observing every move from around the corner in the hallway. He hadn't needed to go to the bathroom at all. Teddy allowed his mother another second or two of looking Micah over. He could tell precisely what she was thinking by the way she was sizing him up. A minute later Teddy entered the room, playing it cool and smooth.

"Hey, sorry about that, dude. You still hungry?" Teddy turned to his parents as he crossed into the kitchen. "Yeah, we haven't had any dinner so I figured we'd come back and I'd make us some of those Salisbury steak frozen dinners." Teddy opened the freezer. "I hope you like au gratin potatoes, dude. Don't worry, I'll scrape the frost off 'em for ya. Mom, Dad, you guys go to bed. We'll be all right."

"Close the freezer door," Mrs. Anderson said.

Teddy ignored his mother and stuck his head in the kitchen cupboard. "Hey, dude, you want a salad? Well, we don't got much, but I could bust you open a can of peas. I don't think they've expired yet."

"I said, close the freezer door," Mrs. Anderson repeated in a low but fierce tone. "This boy will not be eating any freezer-burn potatoes with a can of peas. Tonight"—she paused—"he gets my special chicken."

Pops nearly collapsed. *Did she just say she was gonna make her special chicken?*

"Ya'll go into the other room and watch the basketball game. Dinner will be ready in one hour and fifteen minutes."

"Naw, Mom, you don't have to go to any trouble. We don't mind heating up a few—" Mrs. Anderson shot Teddy a look that could have burned a hole through a steel vault. She knew what Teddy was up to. She saw through his scheme. And while she had just agreed to play along with Teddy's game, she was not about to allow him to act all innocent about the fact that he had just brought home a hungry little foster boy and dangled him in front of her like some sort of desperate charity case who needed a hot meal.

Mrs. Anderson crossed the room, grabbed the two Salisbury steak dinners from Teddy's hands, and dumped them into the trash. Teddy knew better than to utter another word.

Three minutes later, Mrs. Anderson, wearing an overcoat and boots, grabbed her purse and car keys and headed out the front door. Pops turned to Teddy. Their eyes met for the first time in months. Then Teddy cracked a sly smile. Pops smiled back.

"Come on, dude," Teddy said to Micah. "Let's see who the Lakers are playing tonight." They made their way to the couch. Teddy clicked the remote control, and the three men settled in to watch some hoops.

19

One hour and sixteen minutes later, Mrs. Anderson called all three to the table. Though it had been a while since she had taken to the kitchen, just one look at the feast she had laid out showed that she hadn't lost her magic touch. Chicken, garlic mashed potatoes, roasted corn, fresh biscuits, oven-baked yams—it was a banquet from paradise. When Pops saw the spread, he began to salivate so much he had to swallow a big gulp so that drool wouldn't dribble down his chin.

Pops took his seat at the head of the table, grabbed the salt, and began to lick his chops. Mrs. Anderson shot him a glare. With his history of hypertension, Mrs. Anderson wasn't going to tolerate Pops salting his food. Pops slowly set the salt shaker back down without an argument. He wasn't about to do anything stupid to jeopardize this meal.

Pops grabbed a biscuit and shoved the entire thing in his mouth like a sideways slot machine sucking up quarters. Micah politely unfolded a napkin and put it on his lap. Then, while still chewing, Pops slapped a spoonful of mashers on his plate, grabbed a drumstick, two thighs, and a chicken breast, licked his fingers to taste his wife's special homemade barbecue sauce for the first time in what seemed like forever, and gulped down a second biscuit.

"Mmm-mmm!" Pops exclaimed, heading for the yams.

Everyone started making a plate for themselves. Everyone except Micah. "Something wrong, dude?" Teddy asked.

"No, I just . . . well . . . would it be 'kay if I said grace?" Micah said. The table froze. "I mean, I ain't really had a meal like dis since way back when, like when I used to go to church and all, and—well, I'd kinda like to say thanks if that's okay."

Pops, with his face full of biscuit, crumbs on his chin, and his fingers covered in sauce, paused. Mrs. Anderson shot her husband a disapproving look.

"Of course it'd be okay, honey," Mrs. Anderson said to Micah. "Matter of fact, it sounds like a nice idea."

Micah bowed his head. Everyone else followed his lead. A moment passed in silence.

"Amen," Micah finally said.

"Amen. Amen. Amen," said Mrs. Anderson, then Teddy, then Pops in turn.

Everyone dug in. As the meal wore on, Micah surprised the heck out of Teddy. It turned out he had excellent table manners, which Teddy thought the boy must have learned at those church dinners. Not once did he chew with his mouth open, put his elbows on the table, or use his shirt sleeve for a napkin. Micah even used a fork to eat his drumstick.

On the other hand, Teddy's father made small snorts as he gobbled down food, never once used his fork—not even for the mashed potatoes, which he guzzled up using broken-off pieces of biscuit—and chewed with his mouth open the whole meal. Plus, Pops splattered barbecue sauce everywhere. Everywhere! On the tablecloth, the floor, the legs of his chair. By the time the meal was over, Pops had even splattered sauce in his hair.

"*Bu-u-rrph!*" Pops belched. His stomach was so full, he had to unbutton his pants. "*Mmm-mmm*, that was good. I couldn't eat another bite."

"Did you get enough to eat, child?" Mrs. Anderson asked Micah. "How about another wing?"

"No, thank you, ma'am. I'm full."

"Well, I hope you saved room for dessert. You do like chocolate cake, don't you?"

Pops's eyes suddenly lit up. *Please like chocolate cake, boy. Please like chocolate cake.*

Micah looked at Pops before he answered. "Yes, ma'am, I like chocolate cake."

Yes! I like this boy!

"But you don't have to go to any special trouble for me, ma'am. Really, you've already done enough."

No! Shut up, boy! Shut up! Let her go to the trouble!

"It's no trouble, honey. It'll just take a little bit. Why don't ya'll go inside and watch the rest of the game, and I'll make us some dessert."

"Now that's what I'm talkin' about," Pops said, leaping out of his chair. "Come on, Micah. Hoop time!"

Pops headed for the living room, but Micah didn't budge. Instead, he turned to Mrs. Anderson.

"Would you like some help with the dishes, Mrs. A.?" Micah asked. "You shouldn't gotta do all the work by yo'self."

Pops stopped dead in his tracks, already halfway to the television set.

"No, thank you, Micah," Mrs. Anderson said, thinking that her husband sure could learn a lot from this boy. "You go watch the game."

"Come on, dude," Teddy said. "I'll call Diaz and tell her what's up, and that you're gonna stick around and watch the fourth quarter with us." Teddy led Micah to the living room, grabbed the cordless phone, flopped onto the couch, and clicked on the television set.

Pops eyed Micah as he walked across the living room. *Barbecued chicken. Chocolate cake. The basketball game.*

"Would you like to sit in my chair, son?" Pops asked Micah. Teddy looked up in shock. In all the years Pops had been sitting in that chair, Teddy had never seen him offer it up once to anyone else.

"No, thank you, Mr. A. I'm fine next to T.B."

"Z.D.? What the heck is a Z.D.?" Pops asked.

"T.B., Pops. It's what he calls me," Teddy said. He turned to Micah. "You kinda got to speak toward his left ear a bit. He's a little deaf."

"Well, have the boy call me Pops," Teddy's father said, taking a seat in his chair. "Ain't nobody calls me mister anything in my own home."

Micah took a seat on the couch. When Teddy kicked off his shoes, Micah kicked off his. When Teddy put his feet on the coffee table, Micah put his feet up too. And when the Lakers scored on a three-on-one fast break that ended in a ferocious slam dunk, Teddy high-fived Micah with a loud *smack!* that hurt Micah's hands, but brought a smile to his face.

"Hey, boy, can you do me a favor?" asked Pops at the next commercial break.

"Sure, Mr. A—I mean, Pops. Wuzzup?"

Pops pointed to his right foot. "Just pull on that big

204

toe right there. Got me an ol' injury that's kinda stiff. It's tough for me to reach."

Micah looked at Teddy, who just shrugged as if to say, *I don't know.*

"Just give it a little pull, would ya?" Micah leaned forward and reached out to tug gently on Pops's big toe. "A wee bit harder now, boy." Micah pulled harder. *Ri-i-i-i-i-p-p-p-p!* Pops blew out the loudest fart Micah ever heard.

"Thank you, boy, appreciate it," Pops said, relaxing back into his chair.

Teddy instantly covered his nose with his shirt and broke up in laughter. Pops had nailed Micah with one of the oldest tricks in his book. A moment later Pops began to laugh too—and farted again. Micah looked around, then smiled, quickly covering his nose with his shirt just like Teddy.

"Dang, it smells like wet cheese," Micah exclaimed.

"Willard!" Mrs. Anderson called out from the kitchen. "Don't be making that boy pull your toe!"

Pops chuckled heartily, then farted a third time.

"Dang, son," Pops said with an easygoing smile, "we should have you over every Tuesday night."

And that's exactly what they did. Tuesday night became "Micah night." With Diaz's blessing, Teddy helped Micah with his homework, then they watched a basketball game while Mrs. Anderson cooked up a feast.

Three weeks later, during the halftime of a tightly fought Lakers–Celtics game, Micah excused himself to use the bathroom.

"Hurry, dude, I got a feeling this game is gonna come down to the last shot."

"And dessert is next," Pops added, excited by the thought of homemade peach pie with vanilla-bean ice cream.

Micah zipped down as fast as he could, opened the door, clicked on the light, then turned to lift the toilet seat. All of a sudden he realized his mistake.

Micah looked around in amazement. There were pictures of eighth-grade graduation, trophies won for academic excellence, and fluffy pink pillows on the neatly made bed. The space was like a shrine, seemingly untouched since her death. Micah opened the small jewelry box. It played a girly-sounding song when he lifted the top. As he took in all of the room's details he realized that Tina had been a good student, a nice person, and smart. She must have been the perfect daughter, Micah thought.

"Micah, come on, dude. Pie time!" Teddy called

out. Micah softly closed the door, went to the bathroom, then rejoined Teddy and Pops. The Lakers won in overtime, but Micah hardly watched. Mrs. Anderson served him a hot slice of pie with the crust nicely browned, just the way he liked it, but he only nibbled at it. Aside from a polite thank-you to Mrs. Anderson and Pops as he left for the evening, Micah barely said a word the rest of the night. The Andersons, of course, noticed that something was wrong, but nobody wanted to pry.

Teddy drove Micah back to his foster home just as he had been doing for the past few weeks. They rode in silence. As they neared Micah's neighborhood, Teddy made an effort to lift his spirits.

"Dude, I can't tell you how much my folks like you." There was no answer. "I mean, I know you've only been over a few times, but I'm telling you, it's the highlight of my parents' week."

"T.B., I gotta tell you somethin'."

"What? You hooked up with that girl Zayra you was talking about? Told you she'd be into you, dogg. Take it from the master. Girlies love a man with confidence."

"Naw, T.B., ain't nothing like that. This is serious, homie."

"Wassup?" Teddy asked.

"You ain't gonna be mad, is you?"

"What is it, dude?"

"First you gotta promise that you ain't gonna be mad."

"I'm not promising anything, Micah. Just tell me what you got to say."

Micah paused. "Like, I don't really be knowin' how to tell you this and all, but you know that dude Maggot? He ain't the one that blasted yo' sista."

Teddy immediately pulled over to the curb and stared at Micah.

"It wasn't O-One-O at all, T.B. Homeboyz who did it, they was from Serpent Street."

20

Serpent Street was another one of the neighborhood's most vicious gangs. Murder, violence, drug dealing, weapons—if it was illegal and profitable, Serpent Street had their fingers in it.

Their gang sign was two intertwined capital letter S's interlocked like a pair of venomous snakes mating. Terror filled the hearts of anyone who saw their spray paint around their neighborhood.

The mainhead shot-caller of Serpent Street was a twenty-four-year-old crime prodigy named Eevil, a fourth-generation gangbanger whose mother had given birth to him in jail. Eevil was ruthless, intelligent, and highly ambitious. He was also Micah's second cousin, the one Diaz had mentioned to Teddy a few months prior.

As Teddy sat parked on the side of the road, he listened to Micah explain what had really happened that day in the park. Eevil had spent weeks setting up an elaborate scheme that would frame the 0-1-0's for the murder of a 22nd Street Merk in order to get those two gangs to go to war. A bitter war between Eevil's two fiercest enemies would allow Serpent Street to expand its drug trade while their neighborhood drug-dealing rivals spent all of their energy trying to battle one another. The plan had worked perfectly. Shooting an innocent bystander while blasting a 22nd Street Merk had in fact been a deliberate tactic to rile up the police and draw extra heat to the 0-1-0's.

At first, the 0-1-0's denied the shooting, but the more they claimed that it wasn't their fault the more Eevil had his street soldiers spread the word that the 0-1-0's sounded like "weak-ass punks." The question of who had murdered who was quickly lost. And since the Merks were in such a rage and so thirsty for revenge for their fallen homegirl, Blink, they went blastin' at any 0-1-0's they could find, neglecting all rumors that 0-1-0 wasn't really responsible for the drive-by in the first place. Soon the Merks had spilled some 0-1-0 blood, which then needed payback in turn.

Just as Eevil had planned, the situation escalated, and the origin of the conflict didn't even matter any more. It was street war. Merk 22's vs. 0-1-0's. Green lights to blast on sight.

For ten days, Serpent Street had been under strict orders from Eevil to lay low. Then, when Eevil felt the time was right, he began to capitalize on the fresh financial opportunity presented by the ferocious war between his gang rivals. Within three weeks, Serpent Street was selling triple the amount of drugs and handguns on the corners of their neighborhood, while the 0-1-0's and Merks rolled through each other's territory, doing drive-bys and causing mayhem almost every night.

Eevil was smart enough to know that peace on the streets in his area of the 'hood would bring more customers, because people who bought drugs just wanted their drugs; they didn't want to be blasted in random acts of violence in pursuit of getting high. Eevil's territory soon gained a reputation as a safe place to score and get a fair deal. Eevil always made sure that his baggies were weighed, and that his customers were given the full amount of top-quality drugs they were paying for. Just like a great restaurant chef, Eevil knew that outstanding service would result in customer loyalty. Soon enough, Eevil was sitting on enough Benjamins to buy himself a brand new Range Rover—in cash. And even more of the ladies came flocking.

"How do you know all this, dude?" Teddy asked when the boy had finished telling his story.

"'Cause, like I said, Eevil's my second cousin and Serpent Street is the crew I was just 'bout to join before Diaz slapped me with this ankle bracelet, put me on home pro-bay, and busted me in a room wit' you."

Teddy fell silent, lost in thought.

"But you can't be mad at me, T.B. Eevil might be a relative and all dat, but he ain't family, ya know? He jus' a thug, a buster, and only really wanted me to join the gang so I could be used as 'nother one of his punk boys." Micah looked at Teddy. "You my real homeboy, T.B. Please don't be mad."

Teddy didn't answer. He just stared straight ahead. A part of Teddy had somehow thought that this part of his life was over. Now he knew it wasn't.

Teddy put the car in gear and drove Micah to his foster home. The rest of the trip passed in total silence. When Teddy pulled up to the curb, Micah didn't want to get out of the car.

"But you can't be mad," he said.

Teddy reached over, pulled the door handle, and opened the passenger door. "Out."

"Come on, T.B. Don't be like dat."

"I said, out!"

"But why, T.B.? Why?"

"Why?" Teddy replied. "'Cause how long you known about this?"

Micah lowered his head. He didn't answer.

"Yeah, that's what I thought."

"But if they knew I even said shit to ya now, they'd—"

"Out, Micah! Just get the hell out."

Micah paused, then slowly unbuckled his seat belt and began to get out. "But you can't be mad," Micah repeated, tears starting to fill his eyes. "You can't be."

Teddy didn't answer. He just waited for Micah to get out of the car, then pulled the door closed. A moment later, the blue Honda disappeared into the night.

Back home, Teddy headed straight for his computer and logged into CLETS. It took no time at all to find Tyrone Ellis "Eevil" Williams in the system.

Though Eevil had dropped out of school in tenth grade, his rap sheet was short, which Teddy interpreted to mean that he had found a way to get other people to do his dirty work for him. Further investigation into Eevil's academic records revealed that a series of tests he had taken in fifth grade had indicated high academic aptitude. However, his records were littered with behavioral problems. In the words of his sixth-grade homeroom teacher, Tyrone was "defiant, with a streak of unnatural cruelty toward others, particularly weaker kids with no means of defending themselves." Apparently Eevil had been good at inspiring other kids to gang up on his chosen victims. Just as some people were born with the ability to sing or dance, Eevil seemed to have been born with the gift of devious charisma. Clearly, he had always been a leader.

As Teddy thought more and more about Eevil's scheme, he realized how ingenious it was. Media attention would pressure the police to nail someone for the drive-by that had resulted in Tina's death—the wrong perp was better than none. Maggot was the perfect target for the cops to arrest, an 0-1-0 with a rap sheet a mile long. Plus, since Maggot was such a hardcore soldier, the cops knew he would never say a word to any of them—not even to save his own butt. That was the code of the streets. Like so many other gangbangers, Maggot would figure he'd done so much stuff for which he had not been caught anyway, that getting caught for something he hadn't done just went with the territory. There was no need to squawk about getting pinched by the po-po for a crime he hadn't commited, it was just another part of the Game. Maggot knew that if he said anything to the po-po, all the 0-1-0's in jail would suffer, since then other ganged-up inmates would see them as a punk gang full of snitches. If Maggot did yap to the cops, his own gang might have been forced to take him out for their own self-protection. Snitching was the worst crime of all for any crew of homeboyz. It was better to let the cops and courts do whatever they were going to do. Gangsta logic. From the inside, it made perfect sense.

Maggot might have been set up, but his homeboyz would know that he wouldn't say a thing to the cops. That would end up juicing his rep, meaning things behind bars wouldn't be so bad for him. Maggot gained in stature for taking a false rap like a man, and he moved up the hierarchy inside prison as a result. In the world of homeboyz, it was all about the rep. Maggot had proven he was down for the 'hood. That was good enough.

Besides, was a thing like Maggot supposed to give a damn about an enemy like Li'l Gal Blinkie being blasted? Or an innocent girl?

After Teddy had put all the pieces of the puzzle together, the situation became clear to him. What was he going to do?

If Eevil had gone the straight road, Teddy thought, he could have been a corporate executive, taking over weak companies and rising to the top of the business world by Machiavellian means. For that he would have been saluted, maybe even had his picture on the cover of *Forbes* magazine. Instead he had gone the street route, and by every measure of a gangsta, Eevil was a raging success. He had made large stacks of dolla' billz in the drug trade; Serpent Street had risen to unprecedented levels of juice in the 'hood, and most of his enemies had been weakened by going to war against one another, diminishing their ranks, energy, and resources. And never once had any of Eevil's rivals realized that they had been played like puppets.

"Freakin' fools be so stupid," Eevil had once bragged, as Micah looked on, handing ten crisp one hundred dollar bills to two scantily dressed girls so they could go on a shopping spree at the mall. The money was the girlies' reward for having just spent half the night sexing Eevil up. "I am the chess master, and those other niggas be nothin' but my pawns."

But Teddy wasn't so bad at chess himself.

21

The next day Teddy and Micah pretended to follow their regular routine. After a few minutes, Diaz disappeared into her back room to do some paperwork. When the door closed, Teddy turned to Micah. "Who was the shooter?"

"I ain't think you was comin' back."

"I said, who was the shooter?"

"Don't know," Micah answered. "But it wasn't Eevil. He don't do stuff like that unless he gotsta."

Teddy knew Micah was telling the truth. Mainhead gangsters often used young wannabe gangstas looking to make a rep for themselves to do missions for the 'hood. That's because wannabes were disposable. If the wannabes didn't get caught, they'd juice their reps. If they did get caught, most of them didn't have any serious priors anyway, so the law would usually only slap them on the wrist, while a guy like Eevil would have gotten years in jail for the same crime. That was why so many young kids, ten, twelve years old, were recruited with such zeal by gangs. Not only were they naive and impressionable, they made for the perfect message boys and mules. Wannabes would eagerly do risky dirty work in order to make a good impression on the older homeboyz, not suspecting that they were being used. If the wannabes died, they died. And if they went to jail, they had better keep their mouths shut because the gang's retaliation would be far worse than anything a cop could ever do to them. And if the wannabes made it through the mission, they'd get gangsta love.

Gangsta logic. Sometimes it made too much sense.

Micah told Teddy more about Eevil. The mainhead knew that kids with no fathers in their homes and no role models in their lives would line up to follow him like he was the Pied Piper of the inner city. Money, women, cars, clothes, guns—he had it all. And Eevil was one of the most generous gangstas who had ever walked the streets. Instead of telling kids to go to school, he'd encourage little homies to ditch class and come kick it with him and his boyz. "School's for fools, li'l nigga," he'd say. "Here's a twenty. Go run to the market to git me a Gatorade—and get yourself somethin', too. Matter of fact, keep the change. Hell, I got so many twenties, I could start my own line of ATMs."

The kids would always laugh at that last line. Then, when they returned with Eevil's Gatorade and some chips and a soda for themselves, Eevil would pass them a hit of weed and teach them how to draw deep and hold the smoke in their lungs so that they would get super stoned. Soon, when Eevil had gained their trust, affection, and loyalty, he would slap them, bust 'em in the mouth, and make them bleed. He wanted their love and idolization mixed with fear so that they wouldn't dare think for themselves. Soon little homies would do whatever they were ordered.

Micah described how Eevil built up Serpent Street into a small army of fiercely loyal soldiers. Twelve-year-olds eventually turned fourteen. And fourteen-years-olds eventually turned seventeen. Eevil knew that if he could lock enough kids in at an early age, he could build a crew of warriors. As the number of his young recruits swelled, so did his gang's territory.

By starting the wannabes off with warmth, smiles, food, and affection, he lured them into a world from which there was soon no escape. If a kid wanted to pull back from his growing involvement with the gang, who was around to protect him? Once a li'l homie started kickin' it with Serpent Street, he had better stick with Serpent Street, otherwise Eevil would send some of his other boyz off to talk some sense into him—not with words, but with baseball bats and tire chains.

Eventually, a kid either got jumped in and joined the gang or became a victim of the gang: there was no middle ground. Virtually every kid ended up cornered by the same two choices. *You are with us or against us.*

And once a kid joined a gang, there were only two ways out. Jail was not one of them. In prison, a gang-banger was still a member of the gang. Without ties to a gang, it was almost impossible to survive in prison. Option number one was death, and R.I.P. spray painted on the side of some neighborhood wall.

A more appropriate name for option number two—getting "jumped out"—would have been option number one. Anyone who got jumped out was usually beaten so violently that they died. Or else they got killed to reduce the risk that they would turn into snitches. If they were lucky, snitches got stitches. Usually they got coffins. Sometimes their family members died too.

Teddy retraced every step he had taken up until this point. He had assumed that all of this would be ending for him soon. Lie low, do the probation—*Poof! Dis-ap-pear.* How wrong he was.

Midnight struck as Teddy checked in on his Type II Special Services account. No problems there. He then located Maggot through the California Department of Corrections information hub. Maggot had been sent to Chino, one of the toughest jails in the country.

Teddy stared at the computer screen and formulated a new plan.

The first thing to handle was the ankle bracelet. Taking the device off would be easy. Teddy could have done it long ago, but that would have triggered the tamper alert immediately. Where is the weakness? Teddy wondered. He stared at the ankle bracelet's configuration. Hinges. A battery. The homing device by the phone. A-ha, he thought.

Teddy managed to figure out how to send a false signal to the homing system indicating that he was within eighty feet of the homing device no matter where he really went. Twenty-two minutes later Teddy climbed out his window. After softly rolling Andre's old Honda Accord out of the driveway, he turned on the ignition and disappeared into the night. Once again, Teddy was a free man, back to hunting gangstas.

Teddy rolled into Serpent Street territory like a spy on a reconnaissance mission seeking information about the layout of the terrain, the number of enemies he would have to face, and the best strategy as to how to attack. After pulling up across from Domes Park, better known as Dope Park, Teddy killed the lights and started to look for patterns of activity that he could use for his scheme later on.

Teddy watched as a group of three well-coordinated

ten- or eleven-year-olds ran up to the window of a black Ford Mustang and sold the driver drugs. A look to the north end of the park showed a team of two other kids, aged maybe ten or eleven also, sitting idly on a bench, keeping a lookout for cops or enemies. Yet another crew of older kids sat on a jungle gym in the center of the park, smoking a bit of weed, overseeing the base of operations. However, Teddy thought, they probably didn't have any serious drugs or cash on them. Most likely they were just there to provide oversight and muscle in case anybody tried to do anything loco.

Suddenly, there was a knock at Teddy's window. Teddy turned his head. It was Eevil. He must have come up from around the corner behind Teddy's parked car.

"Whatchya want, nigga? Boyz over there'll hook ya up wit' whatever you need. Jus' roll on up."

Teddy paused and stared Eevil deeply in the eye. "They got Gatts?" Teddy asked.

"Why?" Eevil smiled and then cackled a sinister laugh. "You fittin' to go shoot somebody?"

Teddy smiled back. "Yeah, I think so."

"Well, hell yes, they got those, too. Roll on over."

Eevil stuck two fingers between his lips and whistled loudly, three quick, pointed bursts. A moment later, he walked away, disappearing into the night.

A young kid ran over to sell Teddy a gun. "Forty

dolla be the price." The kid opened a handkerchief and held out a gun for Teddy to inspect, but Teddy didn't touch the weapon. He saw no need to put fingerprints where they didn't need to go.

"I want somethin' that ain't been burned," Teddy said—a gun that hadn't ever been fired. Most of the guns sold on the streets had been used in prior crimes. Forensic technology had long been sophisticated enough to trace guns by the marks they left on the bullets fired from them. Anyone possessing a weapon that could be linked with a prior could end up getting pinched for crimes they'd had nothing to do with.

"Dis' thang ain't been burned. Gimme forty dolla'."

Teddy stared directly into the young gangsta's eyes.

"Shit," said the kid, and ran off back to the older homeboyz. After a short conversation, the junior gangsta ran back over to Teddy.

"Be here same time Thursday wit' two hundred dolla'." The kid got ready to dash off, his work done.

"Hey—" Teddy called after him. The Serpent Street messenger stopped and turned. "I'll need two of them," Teddy said.

The kid paused. "Jus' be here Thursday night wit' cash."

Teddy put his car in gear and drove off into the night.

22

Monday afternoon. The clock ticked to 1:30 p.m. Micah and Diaz sat alone.

The clock ticked to 1:35. Teddy still hadn't shown.

The clock ticked to 1:40. Then 1:45. Obviously, Teddy wasn't coming.

"Maybe he just has a cold or something, Micah. You know, the flu."

"Yeah, right," answered Micah bitterly.

Diaz picked up her cell phone and checked for messages. Nothing.

"Did something happen between you two?" Diaz asked.

"Yeah, I trusted him," Micah shot back. "I knew he'd end up bailin' on me. Everyone always be bailin' on me."

"That's no way to talk, Micah. You know better than that."

"I don't know shit, Diaz, other than I can't trust any of ya'. The only peeps who got my back are my homeboyz. I shoulda known dat all along."

"That's not true, Micah."

"Oh, yeah, then where's T.B.? He's gone, and it's all 'cause o' me."

Micah stood up, tossed his color overlays into the garbage, and walked out of the room.

"Micah! Micah, I want you to go home. You are not to go anywhere but home, you understand me?"

Micah threw the hood of his sweatshirt over his head and walked away with his shoulders slumped, not even bothering to turn around.

That night was moonless. Serpent Street graffiti was everywhere. Homies were kickin' it left and right on the front stoop of an apartment building, listening to tunes, smoking weed, and drinking forties, straight out of the bottle.

Eevil took a long drag on his menthol cigarette while a girl climbed all over him. Just another night chillin' in the 'hood.

Micah walked up from out of the shadows. Homeboyz left and right looked him over with distrust, but everyone knew he was related to Eevil, so they let him pass.

Eevil saw his cousin and smiled.

"Where you been, li'l nigga?"

Micah looked around at all the people on drugs.

"Heat been on me big time. Had to lay low, pretend to do some shit in school, ya know how it be." Micah paused. "But I'm back."

"You back?"

Micah paused again. "Yeah, I'm back. Back fo' good."

Everyone knew what that meant. Eevil pushed the girl off his lap, stood up, and started to stretch.

"Well, you know what dey say, you can take the nigga out the 'hood but you can't take the 'hood out the nigga." Eevil laughed. "You think it's your time, Li'l Stoop?"

Micah puffed out his chest. "Bring it."

"So tell me, where you from?"

Micah flashed the gang sign. "Serpent Street."

"I said, where you from?"

"Serpent Street!"

A few gangstas stood up and made a circle around Micah. Though he was small, Micah had a big heart. It was time for him to prove it. The homeboyz started to close in.

"Yo, yo wait a sec. Let me do this bitch one-on-one," came a voice from a few feet away. "I ain't jumped a mo'fo' in for almos' two years and I just be itchin' to deal."

The crowd parted, and a massively muscular

Hispanic gangsta appeared, inked up everywhere. Tatts on his chest. Tatts on his neck. Tatts etched into the back of his bald head. His name was So-Cee-O, and he had just gotten out of jail two days earlier on a legal technicality.

Micah gulped. He knew all about So-Cee-O. Everyone in Serpent Street did. So-Cee-O was a twenty-year-old who'd been kicked, punched, beaten, stabbed, and shot more times than he could remember. And he had done the same to others. His rep on the streets matched every worst nightmare a gangbanger could have.

So-Cee-O's time behind bars had allowed him to get swollen—thickly muscled all over from weight lifting and bodybuilding. He wasn't just a homeboy, he was a human tank. And So-Cee-O liked pain. Pain made him feel good—the more intense, the better.

"Head-up, Little Man. You wanna be Serpent Street—jus' me and you."

Micah's heart started to pound. Mixing it up with five or six members of Serpent Street meant he would have had to absorb only a few minutes' worth of punches and kicks before it was all over. Then the crew would have been hugging him and throwing him a ton of gangsta love.

But with So-Cee-O, things were going to be

different. This beating wouldn't be over until So-Cee-O said it was over. He was half drunk, half stoned, and only two days out of prison; who knew when the punishment would end?

So-Cee-O put down his can of beer and burped. Micah was giving up over a foot in height, a hundred and forty pounds in weight, and eight years in age. But there was no complaining. In gang life you played the cards you were dealt.

Micah wasted no time and leaped at So-Cee-O, catching him on the lip with a right cross. So-Cee-O paused. Then smiled. Blood began to cover his white teeth. "Yeah, dat's what I am talking about," he said. So-Cee-O marched forward like an angry bull. It was the last thing Micah remembered.

Three days later, Teddy sat at his computer, itching with frustration. He had poked into every corner of CLETS he could think to look in, but he still had no idea who Tina's killer was.

Pops approached from behind him, a tired but stern look on his face. "Have something you wanna tell me?" he said.

Teddy looked up, but then looked back down at the computer screen. "No."

"You realize," Pops said, "if I have to make the

choice between having a son in prison or a son in the cemetery, I'll choose jail every time." Teddy didn't answer. "Why haven't you been going to see Officer Diaz?" Pops paused, waiting for a reply. "What? You think she wouldn't call? You've missed almost a whole week"

Teddy stared at the monitor in front of him with a defiant look on his face. "I left messages telling her I was sick."

"There ain't nothing wrong with you."

"Damn place can function without me for a few days, can't it?"

"Yeah, probably so," Pops answered as he started to walk away. "But she left a message for you. Micah's in the hospital."

23

Teddy walked down the hall of the hospital corridor and saw Diaz waiting out front of room 3847. He could feel the heat of her glare from fifty feet away.

"I should report you in violation of your parole right now."

Teddy stopped at the door. He hadn't come to talk about his parole.

"Did you hear me? Right this minute."

"How's he doing?" Teddy asked.

"Well, spending three days without medical attention certainly didn't help the situation," she replied. "Looks like he got jumped on Monday, then ditched school on Tuesday and Wednesday, and finally when he came to the office today I immediately saw that he needed help."

"For what?" Teddy asked.

"For what?" Diaz fired back. "Let's see, for starters, he's got a fractured cheekbone, too many bruised ribs to count, and he's pissing blood. You know, I deal with lots of kids, Teddy, but I gotta tell you something: you might be the biggest piece of shit of them all. How could you rip his heart out like that?"

Teddy didn't respond. He looked her in the eye and took whatever she threw at him without a trace of emotion on his face.

"It's one thing not to get it, but you do. You understand it all, and still things come to this," Diaz said, shaking her head in disgust. "Maybe you were right. Maybe saving a kid like him, a wannabe gangbanger with so many things against him from the start—maybe that was just a pipe dream anyway."

Diaz looked down the empty corridor, but she knew there'd be no visitors for Micah other than the two of them. "I guess I thought helping some of these children was an option. Thanks for clearing that up for me, Teddy. You've saved me years' worth of wasted career time."

"Can I see him?"

"You were the one who told me this program was a stupid idea," Diaz continued. "No money. No support. No assistance from above."

"I'm gonna go in to see him."

"The first rule they teach us on this job is not to care. Don't take it personally. Don't take it home with you, because if you think about it too much, it'll only break your heart." Diaz grabbed Teddy by the arm as he turned to enter Micah's room. "Thanks, Teddy.

Thanks for the cold, hard lesson in reality."

Teddy lowered his eyes toward Diaz's hand, which was squeezing his arm. She released her grip.

"Go ahead," she said, her eyes moist. "Besides, you're the only one he's asked for anyway. Just leave no doubt, Teddy. Leave no doubt."

Teddy paused.

"No doubt about what?"

Diaz reached into her purse and grabbed her cell phone. "No doubt that you're going to be entirely out of his life. There's nothing worse than false hope." They stared at one another. "Know what I mean, T.B.?" she added with a sarcastic emphasis on the "T.B." Without another word, she walked away.

Teddy's best option at that moment might have been to flee. Just because Diaz hadn't arrested him right there on the spot didn't mean she wouldn't send a squad car out later that day once she had filed the paperwork. Teddy liked the idea of living as a fugitive from justice much better than the thought of spending the next eight years in Tehachapi. With a head start and money in the bank, he'd be tough to catch. Taking off made the most sense. But first, he thought, Micah.

The first thing Teddy noticed as he walked into Micah's room was the fresh tattoo on his arm, a picture of two interlocked snakes, the infamous Serpent

Street logo. Micah raised his head. Teddy looked him in the eye. Neither spoke.

Teddy walked around the side of the hospital bed, amazed by how much Micah looked like a little boy, with his head lying softly on the pillow, an IV in his arm, and cartoons playing quietly on the television.

"How you doin', dude?" Teddy finally asked.

"Up yours, Dick."

Silence.

A moment later Micah cracked a smile. Teddy grinned, too.

"I'm-a be all right, ain't I, T.B.? I mean, I ain't gonna die or nothin', is I?"

"Naw, you ain't gonna die, dude." Teddy responded. "Doctor said they might have to cut off one of your balls to prevent an infection, but naw, you ain't gonna die."

Micah's eyes got big as dinner plates.

"Just kiddin', dude. Just kiddin'. They ain't gonna touch your balls," Teddy added with a smile. "Hey, nice ink."

Micah looked down at his new tattoo. "Man's gotta do what a man's gotta do, right?"

Teddy took a deep breath. "Yeah, I guess." Teddy glanced behind him. "Check it out, I brought you something," he said, pushing the door to Micah's hospital room closed with his foot. "But keep it on the down-low or the nurse is gonna freak."

Teddy reached into his pocket and pulled out a Whopper, no pickles, no onions. A gigantic smile came to Micah's face. "Awesome!"

"Sshhh," Teddy said, handing Micah the burger.

Micah tore off the wrapper and took a gigantic bite. "Look, dude, I kinda gotta bounce."

"But you'll stop by tomorra', right?" Micah asked, taking another chomp of his burger.

Teddy paused, thinking about what Diaz had just said to him in the hall. Deep down, he hated the idea of lying to Micah. Up until that moment, he never had.

"Yeah, I'll stop by tomorrow," Teddy said. "Don't worry, dude. I'll see you soon." With a heavy heart, much heavier than he would ever admit, Teddy walked toward the door.

"Hey, T.B . . ." Micah called just before Teddy left the room.

"Yeah?" Teddy said, stopping at the door.

"Mumzy B."

Teddy's forehead wrinkled. He didn't understand.

"Mumzy B. That's your shooter."

Micah then took one more giant bite out of his burger, a happy, satisfied look on his face as a bit of ketchup ran down his chin. Suddenly, Teddy got it.

Micah had joined Serpent Street to get Teddy the name of the person who had shot his sister. Only a homeboy could get that kind of info, and Micah felt proud of himself for obtaining it. In his eyes, he had just completed his first major mission—not for Serpent Street, for Teddy.

Teddy watched Micah gulp down the last of his Whopper and raise the volume on the TV.

Mumzy B., thought Teddy. He had never even heard the name.

Instead of finalizing his escape plan Teddy went home and logged into CLETS to research the gangsta with the a.k.a. of Mumzy B.

There was only one Mumzy B in the system and, except that Mumzy B was a few years older, his profile read like a carbon copy of Micah's. He had terrible grades, two older brothers in jail, a rap sheet that included more than twenty criminal offenses, and a home life riddled with abuse, drugs, and instability. When Mumzy B was in second grade, one of his uncles had been shot in a domestic violence incident. When Mumzy B was in third grade, he was called to testify as a witness in court against his methamphetamine-dealing grandmother. When Mumzy B was in fourth grade, he was removed from his foster home and sent to live in a new state home for boys because the woman who was supposed to be caring for him was spending his food money on crack cocaine. In fifth grade, Mumzy B was fitted by the police in his first pair of handcuffs. He'd been wearing them off and on ever since.

The more Teddy read about this homeboy, the more he recognized a familiar pattern. Kids living in poverty, kids underperforming in school, kids being bounced around from home to home, then kids finally turning into homeboyz in a quest for protection, a sense of belonging, and gangsta love.

Mumzy B's real name was Terrence DeMarco Jefferson. Curiously, Mumzy B's a.k.a. had a meaning that Teddy would never have guessed: "Momma's Boy."

Teddy shook his head. A kid without a mother being nicknamed Momma's Boy? Damn, this fool must be soft as jelly.

Just then, Teddy's mother walked into the room. She saw Teddy on the computer and glanced at the screen. Mrs. Anderson was a smart, educated women who knew her way around the Internet, and she could tell right away that her son was on a Web site he shouldn't have been looking at.

Yet instead of saying anything, instead of chewing him out, biting his head off, or really letting him have it the way only a mother could—the way she always had before with all of her kids—Mrs. Anderson continued into the kitchen, poured herself a glass of water, and swallowed her evening pill.

Teddy thought about his father. It was only 8:45 and he was already fast asleep. Teddy twirled back around in his chair. A moment later he opened the desk drawer and reached into the back, finding exactly what he had expected to find.

A small bottle of vanilla-scented hand lotion.

Teddy unscrewed the cap. Memories of Tina flooded his mind. Her smile. Her kindness. Her optimistic attitude no matter how bleak things looked. The only time Tina had ever really cried was when she was feeling sadness for others. If things weren't working out well in her own life, Tina never got down about it, she always forged on. But if things weren't working out well in the lives of the people she loved, Tina would cry and pray and do anything she could to make that person feel better.

Teddy looked back to the computer screen and stared at the online mug shot of Mumzy B, the scent of vanilla hand lotion still filling the air.

Two minutes later Teddy went into his bedroom and dug into the bottom of his underwear drawer, lifted up a false panel, and took out a yellow envelope. Though the envelope was old, the hundred-dollar bills were new and crisp. Teddy peeled off four of them and grabbed the keys to the Honda. In minutes the car was rolling out of the driveway and headed toward Serpent Street. His order for two Gatts unburned— would be waiting.

24

The following Tuesday when Micah got out of the hospital was one of the most exciting days of his life. His cheek still showed signs of swelling and his ribs still ached, but no amount of physical pain could squash the thrill he felt from being a secret agent. Micah was a member of Serpent Street, but in his heart he was Teddy's homeboy. And Teddy hated it.

"Aw, you know I ain't really down wit' the Serp," Micah told him. "Those fools ain't nothin' but a bunch o' punks."

Teddy had indeed shown up the next four days at the hospital to visit Micah. He had not *dis-ap-peared*. Though he had planned on bailing out, on leaving everything behind—all the smacked-up things at home, all the trouble with the law, all the gangstas in the 'hood—something kept him coming back to that hospital room. Returning to visit Micah was a gamble, with very low odds and extremely high stakes, the kind Teddy hated. But Diaz had not reported him and sent him to face Judge Lynch, even though she must have thought of doing so about ten thousand times.

That afternoon, Teddy and Micah sat in the Hawkins Middle School Probation Office at the same old table at the same old time, but everything else was different.

"I mean, why they wanna bring me in, treat me like a piece o' shit, and den get me either dead or in jail? Dat's all homeboyz like that do anyway. I'm just gonna be chillin' with the Serp till we can smoke that fool Mumzy B."

"Shut up, Micah."

"Why? We need to work this out, T.B. Diaz ain't gonna hear. She back there stressin' over paperwork as usual," Micah said with a look toward the back room. "Dude, you know that blastin' be the only thing these niggas—I mean fools—understand anyway. It comes out da' barrel of a Gatt. *Ba-blam!*"

"Micah, I'm warning you. Shut up."

"Aw, you know as good as me da' Bible say an eye for an eye. Vengeance be the only thing these bitches comprehend."

"I said, shut the fuck up!" Teddy bellowed, jumping out of his chair. "Do you know what kind of stupid-ass fool you sound like?"

Diaz popped out of her office. "Is there a problem?"

Teddy turned away, a burning glare on his face.

"No," Teddy and Micah answered together.

A moment passed. Diaz hadn't heard the conversation. "I sure hope the two of you are using your brains in here," she said. Then she went back to the stacks of paperwork on her desk.

"Think about your mother, T.B.," Micah said softly as soon as Diaz had exited. "Look at what Mumzy B did to her. You know, I ain't never had a mom like dat, but if I did and someone hurt her the way Mumzy B hurt yours, I sure as hell'd make things right." Teddy sat with an emotionless look on his face. "Ya owe it to her, T.B. It's the code of the streets. You gotta make things right. Shee-it. I already set it up."

"You did what?" Teddy asked.

"Well, you always tellin' me how I gotta be a leader and not a follower, so I done some leading."

"What'd you do?"

Micah paused.

"I said, what'd you do?" Teddy repeated, a deep growl in his voice.

"Found out where Mumzy B be kickin' it and got a message to him that he gotta do a big mission for Eevil. And he better be there."

"Micah, you are screwin' around with boyz that will—"

"Don't worry, T.B., I worked it all out. See Mumzy been *way* outta touch with the Serp ever since Blink the Merk got blasted, and rumors be startin' to flow that he done lost his nerve and might turn *el ratón* and snitch to the cops, den try to go kick a new life for himself somewhere."

"How you know all this?" Teddy asked.

"The streets gots ears, T.B. The streets gots ears," Micah answered. "Now all you gotta do is show up at dis address tonight at ten." Micah slipped Teddy a piece of paper with an address written on it. "He'll be waitin' for a blue Honda to take him to the ol' rivah'. Once you got him there—*pop-pop!* Do this fool and ain't no one ever know nothin' bout what happened. He'll just be anotha' dead banger left for the rats to eat. Shit like this happens 'round dis 'hood once a month."

"I don't like all this whispering," Diaz said, suddenly popping out of the back room. "What's going on?"

Neither of them spoke. Diaz looked at Micah. He lowered his eyes. Diaz turned to Teddy. It took her less than three seconds to realize there'd be no way to get a word out of them. It was like talking to two concrete walls.

"So that's how it's going to be, huh? All right, time's done. Out! I am not going to stand for any scheming in my office, and I know you two are up to something. And consider the rest of the week canceled, too. Go home and chill out. We'll do more hours next Monday, when homework and positive things can happen in this room. Until then, say goodbye, gentlemen, 'cause you won't be seeing one another for another five days."

Diaz went to the door and opened it for them both to leave.

"Well . . ." she said with fire in her eyes. "I'm waiting."

Thirty seconds later, Teddy and Micah were headed off in separate directions.

Teddy walked through the front door. "I've asked your father for a divorce," Mrs. Anderson said matter-of-factly. She waited for his reaction. None came. There wasn't a hint of emotion on Teddy's face. "We're putting the house up for sale, too," she continued. "I haven't told Andre or Theresa yet. I'll do that next week." Teddy still didn't reply. Mrs. Anderson, assuming the conversation was over, picked up her purse and car keys.

"Micah won't be coming tonight," Teddy said as she was leaving for what Teddy assumed was a supermarket shopping trip.

Mrs. Anderson stopped and turned. "Oh," she said softly. It was Tuesday. Micah's coming over for dinner had become a pattern. And though he had missed last week's meal while he was in the hospital, Mrs. Anderson had expected him that night. Though she tried to hide it, she was obviously disappointed.

Mrs. Anderson put down her things, took off her coat, and disappeared into her bedroom.

An hour later Teddy found his father wiping off a wrench in the garage. Pops didn't hear Teddy approach. "Oh," his father said once he saw his son, "didn't know you was here." Teddy looked at all the tools lying on the workbench. "It's good to keep your pliers clean. And ratchets, too. If ya want your things to last in this world, you gotta maintain them before problems start."

"You wanna divorce Mom?"

Pops paused before answering. "You see this wrench here? I bought this wrench in—"

"I said, do you want to divorce Mom?"

Pops set down his rag. "Sometimes there's only so much a couple can go through, son," he replied. "Sometimes, there's only so much."

A single tear began to roll down Pops's face. Teddy's father started wiping the wrench in his hand with more and more vigor, but the tears, once they started, just kept right on coming. Eventually, he picked up the dirty rag to wipe his eyes.

"You didn't answer the question," Teddy said. "Do you want to divorce Mom?"

"Son, I just want the woman to be happy. And if I gotta lose her so that she can find that again, I guess I'm willin' to pay that price."

Pops watched his father take a long, slow, deep breath. Teddy knew it was common for parents who lost a child to gang violence to lose their marriage as well. He had just never thought it would happen to his own folks.

Teddy turned and went back inside.

25

Though he was supposed to go straight to his foster home, Micah took the early afternoon off from school to see what was cookin' over on Serpent Street. The middle of the day was slow and lazy, the streets were quiet.

Beep-beep. Micah turned. It was So-Cee-O honking at him from behind the wheel of a brand-new Lexus. "Get in."

Micah paused, then did the only thing he could: he got in. The Lexus had a sunroof, a mahogany dashboard, and leather seats. "This yo' ride?" Micah asked.

"Is now," So-Cee-O replied with a chuckle. "I saw this baby and jus' knew I had to creep up on the white dude driving it, know what I mean? Yo, lemme see, Li'l Stoop," So-Cee-O said, pointing at Micah's cheek. The boy's face was still bruised and tender to the touch. So-Cee-O grabbed him roughly, looked over the damage, then slapped Micah hard in the stomach. The stomach slap hurt, but So-Cee-O meant it in a playful way. "Aw, you all right, nigga," So-Cee-O said with a smile. "Hey, that's the man I'm lookin' for right there."

246

So-Cee-O made a quick right turn. Across the street, Eevil sat in a black Chevy with two other homeboyz. When So-Cee-O pulled into the alley, each of the gangstas flashed their signs in a gesture of unity, then Eevil climbed into the front seat of So-Cee-O's Lexus.

"This yo' stop, Li'l Stoop," So-Cee-O said to Micah. "Me and Eev gots to chat. Out."

Micah opened the door, but Eevil stopped him. "Naw, he's cool. Jump on in the back, li'l nigga. We relations."

So-Cee-O hesitated. Whatever he had to say, he didn't want to say it in front of Micah.

Eevil stared at So-Cee-O. "I said, we relations," he repeated with an edge in his voice.

Eevil and So-Cee-O stared each other down. So-Cee-O was the bigger man; but, as an old saying goes, sometimes it isn't the size of the dog in the fight that counts, it's the size of the fight in the dog. So-Cee-O lowered his gaze. Micah did what he was told and jumped into the backseat.

"Hell," Eevil added, "Li'l Stoop might even run the whole show one day—if he can ever learn to read, that is." Eevil let out a laugh and So-Cee-O chuckled. "Naw, just playin' wit' ya, homeboy. Yo, So-Cee, where you get these wheels?" Eevil asked.

"Pizza Hut," he answered, pleased with his own cleverness.

"Fool, this car has way too much flash goin' on. You gonna have the po-po all over you if you don't dump this thing. Take it to D'Podesto's."

"Dude, that fool never pay top dollar for hot rides."

"Just take it to D'Po-fucking-desto's," Eevil ordered.

Again, So-Cee-O lowered his eyes and agreed to do what he was told. There could only be one mainhead shot-caller in any gang, and Eevil made sure that message was clear to every soldier in his Serpent Street crew.

"So what's so major you gotta call me three times on the cellie in one afternoon?" Eevil asked.

So-Cee-O hesitated. "A li'l squirrel told me Mumzy B wants out."

Eevil took a moment to digest the information. "Fo' sure?" he asked.

"Solid," So-Cee-O replied. "Got it from a ho I know who is cousins with a girl he be runnin' with." Eevil sat for a moment in silence, looking troubled. Micah sat in the backseat, not saying a word. "So, we gonna violate this fool out?" So-Cee-O asked.

"Bitch could snitch and bring down all these riches," Eevil said aloud, more to himself than to anyone else.

"Yeah, and we been makin' nothin but large dolla'

billz for months. Gotta admit, Eev, you the man wit' the plan."

"And I sure ain't about to let this one fool punk us out."

"Ya' think he'll snitch?" Micah blurted out from the backseat. Both Eevil and So-Cee-O turned around and glared. Micah's job was to sit still and shut up. Eevil debated backhanding him across the mouth with the hand he wore three rings on, but he didn't.

"The question be, am I willin' to take the chance?" Eevil answered, turning back to So-Cee-O. "'Cause I sure ain't chancin' going back to the pen again."

"What's wrong with lockup, homie? Hell, sometimes, when the shit be getting' all crazy, I kinda like it in there," So-Cee-O said.

"Not me, homeboy. I like my freedom," Eevil said.

"Me," So-Cee-O answered, "I just like action, wherever it be." There was a pause. The engine of the Lexus hummed quietly. "So what you wanna do?" So-Cee-O finally asked.

Eevil took a moment before replying. "Green light."

The words sat in the center of the car like a black cloud. Then So-Cee-O smiled, big and wide.

"I'm puttin' a green light on Mumzy B," Eevil repeated.

Holy shit! Micah thought. *Green light* meant they were going to kill him.

"What you think about that, Li'l Stoop?" Eevil asked.

Micah hesitated. He knew there was a lot riding on his answer. "I think, if da' bitch gonna snitch we blow his fuckin' brains out," Micah said at last.

A slow smile came to Eevil's face. He turned to So-Cee-O. "Told ya, that's my homeboy."

"Solid," agreed So-Cee-O with a nod. "Very solid, Li'l Stoop."

Eevil climbed out of the car. "Now go dump this thing before the po-po bust ya. And take care of that otha' shit by midnight tonight. When I want somethin' done, I want it done 'mediately."

"Gonna be my *pleasure*," So-Cee-O replied, beaming.

Eevil jumped out of the car, followed by Micah. So-Cee-O burned rubber and tore away.

"Fool," Eevil said as smoke came from the back tires. "Jackin' a car like that just to cruise 'round, brings a homeboy too much heat."

The doorbell rang. Mrs. Anderson answered, and found Micah shivering before her. "I . . . I didn't think you were coming tonight."

"I hope it's okay, ma'am. I mean, I could leave."

"No, no, come in, Micah. Come on in, child." Mrs.

Anderson pulled Micah into the house and closed the door behind him. "Come in and get out of that cold."

Teddy appeared in the hallway. He stared at Micah long and hard.

"I thought you said he wasn't coming this evening," Mrs. Anderson said.

Micah answered before Teddy had a chance to speak. "And miss a meal cooked by you? Aw, heck no, Mrs. A. Eatin' hospital food last week was bad enough, but two Tuesdays in a row, ain't no way. Took me three buses to get here."

Teddy continued to glare. Mrs. Anderson could tell something was going on. She looked at Micah's cheek, still swollen. Now that he was in her house, Mrs. Anderson wasn't about to let him out, at least not without a home-cooked meal in his stomach.

Mrs. Anderson grabbed her coat and car keys, glowering at Teddy.

"I'll be back," she said. A moment later, the front door closed behind her.

"Yo, we gotta talk," Micah said.

Teddy grabbed Micah by the front of his sweatshirt and pushed him up against the wall.

"It's a green light! It's a green light!" Micah cried defensively.

"Green light on who?" Teddy asked.

"A green light on Mumzy B. Dey gonna do it tonight at midnight."

Teddy released his grip and then walked away into the living room.

"It's now or nevah', homie."

Teddy sat on the couch, staring into space. "You sure they going to ice him?" he said.

"Pos-i-teev-o," Micah replied.

Teddy weighed the situation. Micah didn't understand his hesitation.

"What's up, T.B.? I mean, think about your sister."

Teddy raised his eyes and scowled.

"Think about your mom."

"Shut the fuck up, Micah!"

"What?" Micah responded. "I just don't get why you ain't wit' this."

"Because we're talking about murder. We're talking about killing somebody!"

"Yo, it ain't murder. It's revenge. They totally different," Micah answered.

Teddy collapsed onto the couch. Micah grew more and more impatient. "Dude," he said, "I just don't get you. We got dis fool. We gots him wrapped like a Christmas present. What is up?"

Teddy shook his head. "He's gonna get capped anyway."

"So . . ." Micah said.

"So," Teddy replied, "so then why do I need to do it?"

"Dat's exactly why you need to do it! So you can put dis baby to bed. How many mo' nights ain't you gonna sleep, T.B.? Schoolin' this fool is the only way to put your mind at rest."

Just then Pops walked in, startled to discover Micah in his living room. Teddy raised his eyes to look at his father. Pops stared back at him as if he could read his mind. Pops knew the two boys were up to no good. A man didn't get to be Pops's age and not know trouble brewing when he saw it, especially when it involved his own flesh and blood. "You here for dinner, Micah?"

"Yes, sir," answered Micah.

"You come for anything else?" Pops asked.

Micah hesitated. He had never lied to Pops. And he had vowed that he never would. "Yes, sir," Micah answered. "I had to tell Teddy something important."

"Does this something involve stupidity?" Pops asked.

Micah hesiated again. "Kinda depends on how ya' look at it."

Pops turned his eyes to Teddy. "Well, I guess all boys at some point must become men. Ain't that right, Micah?"

"Yes, sir, I think dat's true."

Pops continued to stare at his son. Teddy didn't raise his eyes to look back at his father. "Call me when dinner's ready," Pops said, then he left the room.

Mrs. Anderson served dinner an hour later. While the food was, as usual, delicious, the atmosphere was tense and almost silent. Everyone at the table was wrapped up in their own thoughts.

Pops excused himself from the table early, passing up dessert. Not long after the boys had cleared the plates, Teddy grabbed his car keys and went to wait by the front door. Micah, stalling for time, brought the last dirty dish from the table to Mrs. Anderson.

"In case I don't see ya' again, Mrs. A., I—I just wanted to say thank you." Micah reached out his little-boy arm to shake Mrs. Anderson's hand. "Thank you very much." Tears started to form in Micah's eyes, but he fought the urge to cry.

Mrs. Anderson didn't shake Micah's hand. She refused to. Instead she hugged him. She grabbed Micah like a package of paper towels and squeezed and squeezed until Micah thought she might break his back. When she finally released him, both of their faces were full of tears.

"Let's go, dude." Teddy said, still waiting by the door.

After one more look at Mrs. Anderson, the kind of

look that a puppy gives to its master before being drowned in a lake, Micah turned around and left.

The drive to Micah's foster home was silent the whole way. When Teddy finally pulled up to the curb in front of Micah's house, he didn't even turn off the engine. "Out," he said.

Micah suddenly reached over and grabbed Teddy's hand, leading it through a complicated handshake followed by a snap and a finger flex.

"What the hell is that?" Teddy asked.

"Serpent Street code," Micah answered. "It's how he'll know you fo' real." Micah repeated the handshake slowly.

When Micah was finished, the silence felt thick and awkward. Teddy finally spoke. "And what about you?" Teddy asked.

Micah shook his head. "Don't know, T.B.," he responded. He smiled. "But I'm sure you'll think a somethin'." Micah jumped out before Teddy could say another word, and disappeared into the house.

Teddy sat silently in his car. He didn't like it. He didn't like it one bit. But for some reason, Teddy couldn't stop himself from pulling up to the address Micah had given him just as the digital clock in his car flipped to 9:57 p.m.

26

Teddy glanced at the gun in his lap, the weapon he had bought from Serpent Street. The Gatt was clean and new, shining silver in the moonlight.

A moment later an apartment door opened, and a boy who looked about sixteen appeared. His head was shaved, he wore an oversize white T-shirt underneath an oversize hoodie sweatshirt and baggy jeans that sagged around his waist. The classic gangbanger outfit.

The boy's eyes darted around as he walked up to the Honda. He nodded. Teddy paused, then nodded back. A moment later Mumzy B opened the door and climbed into the front seat.

"What up, dogg? Mumzy," the boy said, introducing himself. He held out his right hand.

"T-Bear," Teddy responded before leading Mumzy B through the Serpent Street handshake.

"Cool," said Mumzy. "Let's do this."

Teddy went to put the car in gear, when suddenly the door to Mumzy B's apartment building opened again. A young girl appeared. She couldn't have been more than fifteen years old. And she was pregnant. She rushed to the passenger window and gave Mumzy B a frightened but loving kiss. Then she looked at Teddy and whispered something to Mumzy B that Teddy clearly heard. "Promise to be careful."

"I will, bay-bee," Mumzy said. "Now go on, git." She did as she was told. Teddy's stomach sank.

"Come on, let's do dis," said Mumzy B. "Let's do this so I can get the hell back home."

Teddy shifted the car into gear and they drove off. They rode in complete silence for ten minutes or so.

"So, what's the work?" Mumzy B finally asked.

"Just handlin' a delivery," Teddy replied. "You strapped?" he asked.

"O' course, dogg. Got my tool right here." Mumzy B showed Teddy the gun in his waistband.

"That's it?" Teddy replied, a touch sarcastically. "Hell, I always carry one in the belly and one in the back." Teddy showed Mumzy B the gun in his waistband, then leaned forward and showed him the second weapon hidden at the small of his back. "A nigga gotta be prepared," Teddy added.

"I hear dat," Mumzy B responded. "I hear dat."

The car continued on in silence. As Teddy drove out toward the old river he wrestled with what to do. Mumzy B fidgeted in the front seat, clearly suspicious. Teddy had counted on this. "Open the glove compartment," he said.

Mumzy B did as he was told. Inside, he saw two new one-hundred-dollar bills.

"That's your cut," Teddy said, without looking over. "Man's gotta get paid for doin' the work, right?"

Mumzy B hesitated, then relaxed. With a small smile of satisfaction, he took the money and shoved it in his pocket.

"Shit, from what I hear, them diapers gets expensive, too," Teddy added.

"That's what they say," Mumzy B replied. "That's what they say."

Teddy watched Mumzy B take a deep breath then look out the window. He seemed relieved—exactly what Teddy was counting on. Use the money to deflate his suspicion, get him to relax and drop his guard, and then . . . *And then what?* Teddy asked himself. *Then what?*

The car continued along, driving farther and farther away from downtown.

"Got a name picked out yet?" Teddy asked after a while.

"DeMarcus, after my grandfather."

"Gonna be a boy, huh?"

"And I tell you, homie, none of dis gang shit for

him. I mean, I never done had a father. And my moms, she was a strawberry—you know, turning tricks for drugs. Sometimes, she even did the shit in the bedroom right next to where I slept when I was four years old. Naw, little DeMarcus gonna have two parents and a solid home. I'm-a make sure of that. You got any kids?"

"Naw," replied Teddy.

"I tell you, the shit changes you, homeboy. Like all I wanna do right now is figure out some way to get me a job. Problem is, ain't no one want to hire me. Say I got no education. Den they see all these tats and think I'm a fuckin' thief. But I'm a person, you know. I ain't an animal, I'm a fuckin' person." Mumzy B reached into his pocket and took out a cigarette. "Smoke?"

"Naw," Teddy replied.

"Yeah, I gotta give deese things up, too. They'll kill me one day. That is," Mumzy B said with a halfhearted chuckle, "if the Game don't do it first." He lit his cigarette.

Teddy pulled to a stop. "We're here," he said.

The place was desolate. Nothing but abandoned train cars and lines of railway tracks that had sat unused for thirty years. A look of concern crossed Mumzy B's face. Teddy could tell Mumzy's suspicion was starting to grow again.

"We're a few minutes early," Teddy said casually.

"Oh," said Mumzy, taking another drag off his cigarette.

Teddy slipped his hand down to feel the brand new Gatt in his belt.

The quiet made Mumzy B kind of chatty. "Naw, I ain't no thief," he continued as he took another long, slow drag. "I mean, I ain't never stole nothin' from no one unless I was on a mission. Yo, I may be a homeboy, but I got honor."

"If we ain't got honor, then what do we got?" Teddy replied, opening his door to climb out of the car. Teddy jumped up onto the hood and rested his back against the windshield as if he were reclining in a lounge chair.

A minute passed before Teddy heard Mumzy B open his door. The soft crunch of gravel underneath Mumzy B's feet revealed exactly where he was standing. Teddy remained patiently reclined against the windshield, as if he didn't have a care in the world.

"Eevil gonna be out here too?" Mumzy B asked.

"Naw, homie, you know Eevil never get his own hands dirty. We just here to pick up a package for the man, then bring it back to the Serp. You here in case I need some muscle. Fools try to jack me, you blast them, ya hear?"

"I hear."

Teddy waited a bit more, giving time for boredom to set in. Five minutes later, Mumzy B hopped up on the hood beside Teddy and lit another cigarette. Teddy leaned forward. "You never stole nothin', huh?"

"Not a damn thing," Mumzy B replied. "Not unless I was on a mission."

"You know who Meeksha Livingston was?" Teddy asked.

"Never heard of her," Mumzy B replied.

"How about Li'l Gal Blink?"

Suddenly, Mumzy B's eyes lit up. He reached for his gun, but Teddy was too quick and kicked it out of his hand. A second later Teddy was holding his Gatt up to Mumzy's neck.

"Hands on the hood, motherfucker!" Teddy shouted as he started to pat down Mumzy B like a cop.

"What the— You Five-Oh?"

"Naw," Teddy replied. He found no other weapons.

"You Merk Twenty-Two?"

"Naw," Teddy said, putting his gun up to the back of Mumzy's head. With a tug of his sweatshirt, Teddy indicated that he wanted Mumzy B to start walking over toward a deserted storage shed. Mumzy B followed the commands. Once in front of the shed,

Teddy kicked out the back of his knees, crumpling Mumzy B to the ground.

"Then where you claim, homeboy?" Mumzy B asked.

"Don't claim nowhere," Teddy replied.

"What you mean, you don't claim nowhere? Then what the hell is this?" Mumzy B said.

"The name's T-Bear," Teddy answered. "T-Bear *Anderson*."

It took a second for everything to register with Mumzy B. "That other girl?" he asked.

"Tina was my sister."

Mumzy B paused for a moment. His manner suddenly softened. "I respect that."

"What the hell do you mean you respect that? You have any idea the shit you brought to my family?"

"Yo, you may not believe this," Mumzy B said softly, "but I think about that girl every day of my life. I mean, Blink, she was a banger and into all sorts of mess—and if you get into the Game, you know the rules, ya know? But ya' sister, she was just a civilian."

"Then why the hell did you blast her?" Teddy asked.

"Dogg, I didn't even know my own fuckin' name when I did that shit," Mumzy B answered. "Homeboyz had me smokin' sherms laced with PCP all night, getting me juiced up for some sort of secret mission. Then they told me in order to prove I was down for the 'hood, I had to do this thing, claim I was O-One-O, not Serpent Street, and then blast two peeps in the park. They told me they was both Merks. Wasn't till the news stories hit the TV that I found out your sister had nothing to do with the Game at all. They used me like a punk, and I ain't gangbanged a day since."

Teddy stood silently. He could tell that Mumzy B was telling the truth.

"Go 'head, dude, blast me," Mumzy B continued. "I can't handle these nightmares anymore anyway. Shit's just too crazy. Too crazy. Jus' do me a favor though, and take this two hundred bucks and give it to my baby. It's all his daddy got." He reached into his back pocket and pulled out the money that Teddy had given him in the car. "It's all his daddy's got," Mumzy B repeated.

Teddy hesitated.

"Just shoot, dude. End this hell. And may the Lord above have mercy on my soul." Mumzy B crossed himself and prepared to die.

Teddy raised the gun and put it to the back of Mumzy B's head, his finger on the trigger. Mumzy B closed his eyes and waited for the bullet.

Teddy lowered his weapon. "Get up," he said.

"Naw, homeboy, do it. I can't handle livin' no more."

"Just get the fuck up," Teddy ordered. "I'm taking you home."

Mumzy B climbed off of his knees. "Why, dogg? Why ain't you icin' me?"

"'Cause," Teddy said as he threw his gun into the river. "I don't want revenge." Teddy then threw Mumzy B's gun into the river, right after his. "I want something you can't give me."

"What's that?" Mumzy B asked.

"I want my sister back." Teddy turned, walked back to his car, and climbed in.

A moment later, Mumzy B entered, too.

"But you should know," Teddy said as he put the key into the ignition, "Serpent Street put a green light out on you."

"How you know dat?" Mumzy B asked.

"Trust me, I know. And they sent a homeboy named So-Cee-O to do it."

"So-Cee-O?" Mumzy B replied with a surprised look in his eyes. "I thought that crazy fool was in lockup."

"He's out now—and looking for you."

"When? When did this happen?" demanded Mumzy B.

"I don't know, couple of hours ago," Teddy replied.

"Shit, take me home, fool! Take me home *now*!"

27

Teddy sped up to the curb in front of the building. Mumzy B's apartment door was slightly open. A sliver of light crept out from beneath the door.

Mumzy jumped out of the car and rushed to the front door. A trail of blood led to the bedroom. Mumzy followed the wet, red trail.

He stopped.

She lay there dead. His pregnant girlfriend had been shot six times, twice in the belly.

"No-o-o-o-o!" Mumzy screamed as Teddy rushed into the apartment behind him.

Teddy stood frozen in horror. He'd never seen such a sight. Though dead, her eyes were still open. Teddy couldn't help but stare.

Suddenly, the distant sound of police sirens filled the air. Teddy turned his head to look out the front door toward the street. Mumzy B leaped for Teddy when he had his back turned and grabbed the gun from the small of Teddy's back. Mumzy raised the Gatt and pointed it at Teddy. His eyes were red, filled with tears and rage.

"Just chill, dude. Just chill," said Teddy, backing away.

A wild look flashed across Mumzy B's face. He raised the barrel and pointed the weapon directly at Teddy's forehead. Teddy stood frozen.

Then Mumzy B turned the gun, jammed it into his own mouth, and pulled the trigger. The explosion blew the brains out of the back of his skull, splattering the walls with blood. Mumzy B crumpled to the ground, dead before his body even hit the floor.

Teddy stood frozen over the wreckage of the two bodies. The sirens drew near. Teddy knew he had no choice. He quickly grabbed his gun from the floor— covered with his own fingerprints—then ran to his car and drove away.

When the police arrived, nobody had seen nothin'. Nobody had heard nothin'. Nobody knew nothin' about nothin'.

But the cops were good at asking questions. And as it turned out, somebody—though they couldn't say for sure, couldn't be positive—but there was a chance that somebody might have seen a really sweet-looking Lexus.

Forty-five minutes later the police handcuffed So-Cee-O outside a pool hall, where he sat smoking a joint in the vehicle he had carjacked earlier in the day. It would be his third strike under the California penal code. Minimum sentencing requirements meant So-Cee-O would get twenty-five to life behind bars.

The next day at sunset, a crew of Serpent Street homeboyz were kickin' it by the jungle gym at the park, the same place they always liked to chill. Suddenly Teddy emerged from the shadows. None of the lookouts had seen him coming. "You the main-head?" Teddy asked.

Seven gangstas put down their forties and stood up to defend their number one.

"I said, you the mainhead?" he repeated. "'Cause if you are, I'm calling you out as a punk-ass bitch."

Eevil laughed. "Who the hell is dis fool?" He chuckled to his boys. Then he nodded, and a few of his soldiers drew a tight circle around Teddy.

"The name's T-Bear," Teddy replied without flinching. "T-Bear Anderson. You ordered a hit that got my sister killed and I'm callin' you out. Me and you, right now, head up." Teddy paused and looked around. The crowd of homeboyz around him had grown to nine. "Unless you're too chickenshit to fight me one-on-one, and gotta hide behind your peeps here."

The crowd fell silent, waiting for a response. Suddenly a voice rang out.

"Bitch, this is Serpent Street! My man's not only

gonna represent, he's gonna knock you out. Go on, Eevil. Give this punk an ass-whippin' like he never done seen!" Micah jumped into the center of the circle and started pushing the homeboyz away from Teddy. "Show him who we are!" Micah yelled. "Give 'em room, fools! Give 'em room. Eevil 'bout to waste this punk. Back up."

The homeboyz around Teddy began to clear out a circle, a ring into which the two warriors could stand alone and battle like gladiators. The gangsta code of honor demanded that Eevil accept Teddy's challenge and fight him one-on-one. Eevil climbed down from where he sat. *Always represent for your homeboyz.* It wasn't just Eevil who was being called out by Teddy. It was the entire reputation of Serpent Street.

Eevil pulled off his shirt. Underneath his long-sleeve hoodie he wore a thin white tank top. When he cracked his knuckles, his muscles rippled.

"You're cooked, fool," Micah snapped at Teddy. "I said, back up, ya'll. Give 'em space."

The gangstas backed up another two feet, and Eevil approached Teddy. The two stood nose to nose. They were of even height, even weight, and even build.

"Ya' should know before we dance, nigga, I'm a mean, dirty, nasty mothafucka," Eevil growled.

"And you should know," Teddy replied without breaking eye contact, "you're gonna need to be."

Eevil's lips slowly curved into a fiendish grin.

He smashed his head into Teddy's face. A three-inch gash opened over Teddy's right eye, splattering blood. Suddenly, Eevil threw three punches to the body, sending Teddy staggering back, hunched over. The brawl was on.

Serpent Street gangstas started cheering their mainhead on. "Get 'im, Eevil! Kick his ass!"

While everyone's attention was on the fight, Micah slyly reached into his pocket and dialed his cell phone, ringing in code #24.

Eevil landed another punch. Then he raised his foot to kick Teddy in the face. Teddy rolled away from Eevil's boot just in time. The kick missed, and Teddy, with lightning quickness, retaliated with a roundhouse kick that swept around to slash Eevil's right leg out from under him. Eevil crashed to the ground, the back of his head slamming against the pavement.

Teddy jumped up, hovering over Eevil and fired three quick blows—right then left then right—to the center of Eevil's face. When the flurry was over, blood poured from Eevil's mouth. Teddy took a step back—then stepped forward again and fired another flurry—left then right then left—once again to the center of

Eevil's face. Now the blood flowed from Eevil's nose too. The many long nights Teddy had spent shadow-boxing had paid off. Both his hand speed and his punching power were ferocious.

Eevil rose to his feet, staggered backward, and felt the blood gushing down his face. "*Whew!* Got a few skills, don't 'ya?" Eevil said, in mock admiration. Then he reached into his back pocket and pulled out a seven-inch switchblade.

"Now I'm-a carve ya' like a Thanksgiving turkey."

Teddy paused. He hadn't brought a blade. Or pepper spray. Or a gun. It wasn't that Teddy hadn't thought about bringing weapons with him—of course he had—but he had chosen not to. He wanted to settle this one with nothing but the weapons God had given him: his fists, his brains, and his heart.

"*Heh,*" Eevil grunted when he saw that Teddy wasn't going to whip out any weapons of his own. "Didn't think it was gonna be like that now, did ya?"

"Yes," Teddy replied coolly. "I did."

Teddy pulled off his shirt and wound the cloth around his left forearm for protection.

Blood flowed down Teddy's face and over his chest, dripping over his six-pack of abdominal muscles. He took a deep breath and mumbled.

"What dat you say?" Eevil asked.

"I said, *Tina*," Teddy replied, "*this is for you.*"

Instead of sitting back and waiting for Eevil to go on the offensive, Teddy went on the attack. Maybe Eevil would stab him. Maybe Eevil would get in a puncture—possibly two—but Teddy knew that a couple of knife wounds weren't about to stop him from finishing the job he had come to do. Eevil would have needed a bazooka to stop him.

Eevil slashed his knife. Once. Twice. Three times. He made contact, but Teddy fended him off with his protectively wrapped left arm. Eevil's blade tore fabric but not flesh.

Teddy launched a series of shots, striking Eevil in each of the ideal target points. Throat. Bridge of the nose. Pit of the belly. Groin. Teddy then grabbed the hand that held the switchblade and bent back Eevil's elbow with such ruthless force that it snapped like a dry branch from a dead tree. Every homeboy in the circle heard the sickening sound.

The knife dropped with a clink. Eevil pulled his arm into his chest like a small bird with a broken wing.

Teddy boxed Eevil's ears, fired a strike at Eevil's throat, and drilled Eevil with another punch to the bridge of the nose. After a stunned second of silence, the mainhead shot-caller of Serpent Street fell.

Silence. The Serpent Street homeboyz stood frozen in their ring. The fight was over.

But there was no way Teddy was going to be allowed to leave. Not without a major beat-down. Teddy might have whipped their mainhead one-on-one, but this wasn't a movie. The hero would not get to walk off into the sunset. One of the Serpent Street gangstas slipped on a pair of brass knuckles. Another picked up a pipe. They would beat Teddy until he couldn't speak his own name. Law of the streets said they had to. The crowd drew nearer.

"Five-oh! Five-oh! Here come the five-oh!" a voice shouted.

Sirens screamed in the distance. The cops! The Serpent Street gangstas took off, scattering in twenty different directions. Even Micah ran. But not before looking back at Teddy and smiling.

Six police cars rushed to the scene, but by the time they arrived, only two men were left. The first was Eevil, lying beaten in a pool of his own blood. The second was Teddy. He saw no reason to run.

"Put your hands where we can see them. Now!" called one of the cops, leveling his gun at Teddy. Officer Diaz jumped out of a squad car.

Some of the cops tried to give chase to a few of the homeboyz who had scattered. Teddy and Eevil were lined up against a wall and patted down, but the cops found no drugs or weapons on either one, only Eevil's switchblade lying in the dirt.

"Okay, right arm behind your back," an officer said to Eevil.

"What you arresting me for? I ain't done nothin'?" he protested.

"Disturbing the peace," the officer replied, twisting Eevil's broken arm cuffing his hands behind his back. Eevil winced in pain.

"Disturbing the peace?" Eevil breathed through clenched teeth. "Shit, I brought peace to these streets. What kind o' bullshit is this?"

"Just zip your lip, homeboy. You're going down."

"Eat me, pig," Eevil snapped back. "My lawyer gonna have me sprung on bail befo' you even type the damn report. And you, bitch," Eevil shouted at Teddy, who was being handcuffed fifteen feet away. "Yo' ass is done. I'm-a eradicate yo' whole family when I get out."

Teddy smiled. He smiled because he knew there would be no chance of that. Earlier that afternoon, Teddy had logged into CLETS and changed Eevil's official gang affiliation in the computer system. The files now read that Eevil was a member of 0-1-0, not Serpent Street. And when a homeboy was misclassified in the prison system—particularly in the holding tank of a county jail—mysterious things could happen.

An officer tossed Teddy into the back of a patrol car. Diaz jumped into the front seat and spun around. "This is your plan?" she snapped. "Where the hell is Micah?"

"He's gonna be all right, Diaz," Teddy replied. "He's gonna be all right."

Diaz stared at the open gash in Teddy's head. "He'd better be, Teddy." Diaz called out to one of the cops who was standing outside the car. "Officer, let's get some medical attention in here."

Ninety minutes later Eevil was tossed into a holding cell with seventeen other gangstas.

"Disturbin' the peace! Dis' is bullshit!" Eevil shouted at the guards. "I'll own all yo' asses by the time my lawyer gets through wit' you. All y'all's asses!"

Eevil turned around. A gangsta named Goat stared him straight in the eye, mad dogging him. Eevil looked around and suddenly realized he was surrounded by enemies. He'd been thrown into a cell filled with 0-1-0's.

"Dis for our homeboy Maggot, doin' many much days at Pelican Bay." A shank struck Eevil in the gut. Eleven other homeboyz beat, punched, kicked, and stabbed him. Four gangstas made a wall in front of the bars so none of the guards could see what was going on in the cell.

In seconds it was all over, and Eevil was just a carcass on the concrete floor, lying in a pool of blood.

Later that week someone spray painted Eevil's name on a wall in his old 'hood. Underneath his a.k.a. were three letters: R.I.P.

28

Soft clouds floated through a blue sky. A bluebird chirped from a lush green tree. In the distance, a bee buzzed. The smell of Sunday morning filled the air.

Teddy paused, then read the name on the tombstone in front of him: TINA MARYSSA ANDERSON. He began to weep. He wept as he had never wept before, streams of tears racing down his face. It was a beautiful day in a beautiful setting. It was the perfect place to cry.

Mrs. Anderson approached and wrapped her arms around her son.

"I thought we lost you," she said.

Teddy gazed up. "I thought we lost you, too," he replied through his tears.

A small, warm smile came to each of their faces as they hugged.

Andre, Tee-Ay, and Pops walked over. A moment later the entire Anderson family was embracing and crying. Nobody spoke, nobody tried to pull away.

The house had been put up for sale. Mrs. Anderson

had applied for a transfer to another branch of her bank. Pops had sold his business and would think about starting a new business in a new town once he got there. Andre would return to Northern California, to rejoin the love of his life and future wife, Gwen. Tee-Ay would return to finish her undergraduate degree in history at the University of Southern California. After that, she would head to graduate school on the East Coast and look up an old friend named Devon. Mrs. Anderson and Pops had decided to stay together and to move to a quieter city. And they would bring their son with them. Their new son.

Officer Diaz pulled her car up along the cemetery's gravel road. She had a passenger in the front seat.

Micah stepped out of the car wearing a white short-sleeved shirt with a navy blue tie. His pants were too big, his socks were the wrong color, and his oversize shoes made him look like a clown. But this was his Sunday best.

Diaz opened the trunk and handed Micah a beat-up suitcase. Micah took the small bag and turned around. A lump formed in his throat. He tried to swallow, but it was like gulping down a bag of golf balls. Mrs. Anderson approached.

At first she didn't speak, she just stared at Micah as if she were inspecting a piece of rib roast at the market. She looked him up, down, side to side, inspecting his outfit, behind his ears, and down his arm, where she spotted a tattoo only half covered by his sleeve. She reached out and lifted the sleeve to get a better look. There had been a recent addition to Micah's ink.

Instead of two intertwined snakes, the tattoo had been altered to look like a heart. Through the middle, it read LOVE.

"I don't like tattoos," she said. "Don't like 'em one bit."

Micah was slow to respond. "I . . . I ain't plannin' to get no more. Mrs. Anderson. I swear that . . ."

"Don't you call me Mrs. Anderson," she suddenly interrupted.

"I'm sorry," Micah responded. "I mean, Mrs. A."

"Nope, that won't do either," she said. Micah looked confused. "From now on, child, you call me Mom."

Micah looked up, and tears instantly filled his eyes. Before he could even smile, Mrs. Anderson started hugging him so tight that he felt like the cheeks of his face were going to be squeezed off.

Diaz crossed to Teddy and handed him a yellow sheet of paper.

"Community service hours are done. I'll waive the

rest that you owe to the state," she said, looking over at Micah, still locked in Mrs. Anderson's arms. "You're free, Teddy," she added. Micah wasn't the only one who was crying; Diaz's eyes were tearing up as well.

"Aw, don't go all soft on me now, Diaz, and start with the tears," Teddy teased as he took the yellow sheet of paper. "I'm sure Judge Lynch'll probably send you some new meat any day now."

Diaz wiped her eyes with the sleeve of her coat. "Program's been cut," she answered matter-of-factly.

"Cut?" Teddy asked.

"Budget cuts," Diaz replied. "No money for prevention. Plenty for punishment, none for prevention," she said with a shake of her head. For the first time in all the months Teddy had known Diaz, she looked worn out and dispirited.

Teddy turned and watched his mother reach into her purse and give Micah a set of keys so he could place his suitcase inside the trunk of her car. Teddy couldn't help but stare at the youthful eagerness of the boy who once seemed destined for either an early street death or jail. G-PIP, as Teddy knew, had changed not one, but many lives.

A small smile crept across Teddy's lips. He made sure that Diaz didn't see it. She wouldn't be down in the dumps for long, Teddy thought. Not when she got a letter from the Department of Type II Special Services indicating that, upon further consideration, the funding of the G-PIP program had been restored with an endowment of three-quarters of a million dollars.

Micah carefully popped the trunk and loaded his meager belongings into Mrs. Anderson's car. Teddy would use official letterhead, a fake e-mail account, and quarterly financial disbursements aligned to the academic school year to make all monetary deposits look authentic. Diaz would never know.

"Aw, I'm sure things'll work out," Teddy casually remarked. "I mean, they usually do when you look at the bright side, don't they Diaz?"

She paused. "You makin' fun of me, Teddy?"

"Who me . . . *nawww*," Teddy said with a grin. "Just do yourself a favor, though, and change your password. I mean how hard is it to crack the word CHOCOLATE?"

Diaz's eyes got big as baseballs.

"Chocolate?" Tee-Ay called out, overhearing the last part of the conversation as she approached her car. "What's wrong with that? It's my secret password, too." Teddy rolled his eyes.

"Don't you know that you wanna use something hard to figure out, like your birthday?" Pops added as he walked up. "Hey, come here, boy," he suddenly called out to Micah. "Me and you gotta have a chat."

Micah walked up to Pops, his head down.

"I got some questions for you. Number one, you done with drugs?"

"Yes, sir," Micah answered.

"Number two, you done with fools?" Pops asked.

"Yes, sir," Micah replied again.

"Final question, and you best think hard before you answer. You gonna get you some grades?"

"I'm gonna try, sir," Micah replied.

"Don't try, boy: do. People who live under my roof, they *do*," Pops answered.

Micah looked around at all the folks who were staring at him. "Yes, sir," he replied. "Yes, sir."

"And people who live under his roof also know never to pull his big toe," Andre added.

"Too late," Teddy said.

"You mean he already got him?" Andre asked.

"With one of those eye-waterin' blasts. Made me have to leave the damn room," Teddy said with a smile. A grin crossed Andre's face.

"Do we have to talk about farts right now? I mean, come on, we're in a cemetery," Tee-Ay said as she opened her car door. "Yo, Micah, you wanna roll with me?" Tee-Ay asked.

"Nah, let him roll with me," Andre said. "You gonna try to tell him all these lies about USC. This dude needs to learn about the mighty Stanford Cardinal."

"Excuse me, how did your football team do this year?"

"Hoops, bay-bee. It's all about hoops," Andre replied.

While Tee-Ay and Andre argued over who would take Micah back to the city, Diaz pulled Teddy aside.

"So what's in your future, Teddy? Gonna go with your folks? A university? If you want, I could maybe write a letter to the NSA on your behalf and see what can be done," Diaz offered. "Don't get me wrong, not that I need to know as an officer. Just as a—well, you know, I'm just curious."

"Me?" Teddy asked. "Aw, I got big plans, Diaz. Big plans. You should know that."

"I don't think I want to know what that means, do I?"

Teddy slyly smiled.

"Yeah, I definitely don't want to know," Diaz replied.

Everyone climbed into their cars. Andre in his. Tee-Ay in hers. Teddy in his. Micah, not wanting to offend either Andre or Tee-Ay, hesitated.

"If ya'll don't mind, I think I'm gonna roll with

T.B.," Micah said. Both Andre and Tee-Ay looked over at Teddy.

He shrugged. "What can I say? I guess some of us Andersons got it, and some of us don't."

Everyone laughed. "Meet ya'll back at the house."

Pops and Mrs. Anderson waited a moment for everyone to get in their cars, then turned back to Tina's headstone. Mrs. Anderson gently put her fingers to her lips, kissed them, then placed the kiss on the top of the newly engraved marble.

Pops looked over at his kids as they got ready to drive away.

"We did good, baby," Pops said as he hugged his wife. "We did good."

"Well," replied Mrs. Anderson, embracing him, "we did the best we could."